A NEGATIVE RESULT

A PARKER PHOTOGRAPHY COZY MYSTERY

SUZANNE BOLDEN

LAUGHING DEER PRESS

CONTENTS

Chapter 1 . . . 1
Chapter 2 . . . 12
Chapter 3 . . . 19
Chapter 4 . . . 26
Chapter 5 . . . 36
Chapter 6 . . . 44
Chapter 7 . . . 54
Chapter 8 . . . 64
Chapter 9 . . . 72
Chapter 10 . . . 82
Chapter 11 . . . 89
Chapter 12 . . . 97
Chapter 13 . . . 103
Chapter 14 . . . 113
Chapter 15 . . . 121
Chapter 16 . . . 128
Chapter 17 . . . 135
Chapter 18 . . . 144
Chapter 19 . . . 149
Chapter 20 . . . 157
Chapter 21 . . . 162
Chapter 22 . . . 169
Chapter 23 . . . 173
Chapter 24 . . . 179
Chapter 25 . . . 185
Chapter 26 . . . 190
Chapter 27 . . . 199
Chapter 28 . . . 204
Chapter 29 . . . 211

About the Author   217
Also by Suzanne Bolden   219
Also by Suzanne Bolden   221

At first light this Tuesday morning, I took Libby outside for a stroll. I loved this time of day, the quiet broken only by the sounds of migrating ducks and geese rising from the mist hovering over the lake. Our local weatherman promised a stretch of Indian summer for the next few days. Great news because it meant unseasonably warm weather, giving us more time to enjoy the vivid yellows, oranges, and reds blanketing the hills around Harmony before the rains and winds of late fall hit.

This break in the weather also meant that the cookout Scott planned for Saturday might work out just fine. It would probably be the last one we could comfortably spend on the deck high up in the river bluffs. Not that Scott would stop grilling in colder weather, but he'd be doing it in a warm coat and hat, while I waited inside by the fireplace. Our developing relationship was one of the best things that happened following my return to Harmony.

The decision to take over my family's photography studio came at a period in my life when I was weary of the hectic pace of living in a big city. I still had my life-long passion for photography and didn't want to retire. My financial position was such that I chose only the bookings that appealed to me. Commissions like that amazing job in Fiji during one of Chicago's worst winters. What a getaway that was!

Keeping my loft in Chicago, even after remodeling my apartment above the studio was complete, meant I could easily slip away and spend time in the city. I'd taken Scott there just a few weeks ago. We did all the tourist things like the lakefront boat tour, the Field Museum of Natural History, and a walk along Michigan Avenue, aka the Magnificent Mile. We ate our way across town from some of the amazing restaurants right outside my place in River North to the historic restaurants on Taylor Street in Little Italy. A memorable weekend, by any measure.

Was I having an Indian summer in the autumn of my life? Things were great with Scott. I was happy with what we had going. It was refreshingly comfortable.

Maybe that was due to where I was in my life now. My perspective on relationships and a work-life balance had matured along with the turning of all the calendar pages I had witnessed.

The pace of my work in the Parker Photography studio was manageable. Early this fall, knowing my partner Mandy would be out for the birth of her first child, I figured we'd still be okay because of Aunt Ruth's help. But I soon realized how much Mandy contributed to the studio's ongoing success. Her business and marketing skills had proved fruitful over the past months. Our flourishing online presence and the flow of new tourists taking in the fall colors meant we'd be kept busy throughout the fall. We would need more help.

My friend Todd Baldwin and the success of his promotional articles in travel publications was partially the reason for the increased tourist traffic through town. A reporter, blogger, and publicist, he'd first come to Harmony to cover my gallery opening. He returned for a 4th of July getaway with friends and then again Labor Day weekend to do some boating. Todd turned out to be the answer to my employee dilemma.

It wasn't hard convincing him to come work for me. With the ability to continue his own work online, he jumped at the chance to make Harmony his home base. I knew his youth might mean losing him back to the big city, eventually. Small town life wasn't for everyone, but he was eager to give it a try.

Mandy was all for hiring him. They got along great. I welcomed his sense of social media for marketing and the enhanced website designs he suggested.

Aunt Ruth took a little more convincing that we needed to hire anyone. She loved being useful to me and keeping her fingers in the business she had once owned, but I felt I was leaning on her too much. After making sure she understood how much I valued her continued help here, she was okay with Todd being part of our team. After I heard about Todd's visit to Shady Pines for after-dinner drinks, I was sure she was okay with it. I pushed aside a twinge of jealousy thinking only I was their special guest. Now Todd's being invited there looked like a win-win.

Libby tugged on her leash, reminding me it was still too cold for her to stay out long. "Sorry girl. Was I getting all contemplative and ignoring you? Time to go in and warm up."

I took in the studio facade as I turned to cut back across the village square. The original front windows remained, but adding historically correct wooden trim, along with fresh paint job, really made the place sparkle. Sidewalk benches and potted fall mums with dried wheat stalks and sprays of orange bittersweet berries created a welcoming feeling. My second-floor apartment's small balcony was a charming architectural feature. More potted flowers and chair cushions added pops of color. Libby loved to sit up there and watch the comings and goings on the street below.

I was proud to be a part of our Main Street merchants and a contributing member of my small community. Yep, Jacqueline Parker, things are looking good for you.

The interior lights were on because Mandy was prepping for our early trip out to the Frank Lloyd Wright Taliesin estate. "Morning Mandy. Sorry I'm late. Libby and I got caught up in the promises and lures of an Indian summer day."

"Hi Jackie," Mandy said, before awkwardly bending to one side across her protruding tummy to rub Libby's head. "And how's my little girl?" Libby knew Mandy always had treats for her. She promptly sat down in anticipation of one.

"I have yet to get that reaction from her," I said.

"Consistency, Jackie. Just plain old consistency," Mandy said with a laugh. "I think I've got everything we need in the camera case. We'll be able to catch that shot you wanted of the morning sun through the roof transoms at the school there."

"How was your weekend? Did you finish up the baby's room?"

"We did. It feels great knowing everything is ready for little baby Drake," she said. "My due date is three weeks away, but Mom said I came early, so I wanted to be ready in case our little buddy makes an early appearance too."

"You're ready, except for a name. Or have you picked one?"

"Still can't decide that. But I have confidence the best one will come to us when we look in our baby's eyes."

"You will," I said. "You two will make terrific parents."

"Thanks, Jackie." She reached out to give me a hug. "And you're the best for taking me under your wing, Jackie. Now I have a career on top of a family. And I'm glad we're able to wrap up the photography parts of this project. This has been a real learning experience for me."

"I'm so grateful you pushed on through the rough spots. I know some days of photographing at Taliesin got pretty long. The editing and pulling it into a promotional campaign can be worked on when the weather isn't so nice and you're home with your little one. Though I hear new moms have a hard time getting sleep, so I won't expect you to do too much."

"We'll work it out. I really want to continue to stick

with this project through to completion. With Todd being here now, the workload has eased. He's really stepped up. So, all of us aren't as stretched as we were over the summer," Mandy said.

"Now that we have help, we could use more room. I've been getting requests from photographers to exhibit here, but I only have so much space," I said.

"My father-in-law has a great big old house. It's only him wandering around in it." Mandy loved teasing me about Scott. "He seems so lonely. Going to work. Going home. To work. Back home. The guy could use some company and then maybe you could convert the apartment to additional gallery space."

"Oh really? Poor Scott. Stumbling around the place all by his lonesome. He's throwing a cookout this weekend. He'll have company then."

"That's not the kind of company I meant," Mandy said with a wink.

"And soon, his little grandson will be chasing around the place. Did you know Grandpa Scott bought a pack-n-play and lined one entire bookshelf with children's books?" I said to deflect the direction she was going in.

"That's so sweet. I thought we would wait a few years, but nature made its own timeline. Everyone is lending a hand to help us gear up for baby Drake's arrival. My parents are prepping, and so is Matt's mom."

She stretched, bracing her hands on her lower back and carefully arching it. "I'm ready too. You can come anytime now, little guy."

"Let's head out and get this done," I said. Libby understood and parked herself in front of the door. "Not this time, girl. Sorry. No dogs allowed on this job."

e arrived at the back gate to the Taliesin grounds within fifteen minutes. We were meeting Mark Peters, director of the Taliesin Preservation here at the school. This entrance was used by the tour buses that shuttled tourists to and from the visitor center a few minutes away. The Taliesin Preservation group worked diligently to preserve the Wisconsin home of Frank Lloyd Wright. The grounds included the Hillside School, which was started as a coeducational learning and boarding school by Mr. Wright's aunts, Jane and Ellen, in 1887. The original building was gone, but the portion built in 1901 remained. Wright converted it to a school for his architectural students and it's where I would be working this morning.

One big component of our work for the group was to create a transitional morphing of still shots from the past and photographs over the years, including the ones

Mandy and I have been taking. We'll create a video of what work had been done and what still needs doing. This has been a challenge for me and a learning experience for Mandy.

I'd been unhappy with the results of our previous photos inside the school. One problem was the lack of light coming through the unique clerestory style dormers in the roof on the day I took them. Wright designed the roof to maximize use of natural light for the student's work. Organic architecture, I believe it's called. Quite fascinating. Photos of young architectural students from the past showed them working in the natural light. I needed to capture the sun at just the right angle to replicate the idea without much additional editing. Only edit I should need will be to take out current day signage, and things that would be intrusive to viewers and future donors.

Mandy also wanted to get a better angle and reshoot the Romeo and Juliet Windmill Tower, a unique, eye-catching structure high up on the hill behind the school. Wright built it as a way for water to be pumped for his aunt's school and the student housing.

Mark greeted us from his sun warmed bench outside the building. "Morning ladies," he said. "Couldn't ask for a better fall day."

"Hi Mark. I agree. I've been relishing these last warm days."

Mandy tucked her tripod under her arm and slung her camera case over her shoulder.

"See you inside when you're done," I told her.

"I shouldn't be long. I've been looking over the photos I took before and know what changes I want to make. I brought a steadier base to work from this time and I'll be picking a better angle to capture the feeling of distance. The layover on the old photos will work better with these changes."

I liked that about Mandy. She studied and considered what she wanted out of her photography. Even though things were digital now, which meant taking, processing, and storing photographs incurred much less expense than in previous times, she still worked to use her time efficiently and not take endless photographs. Shooting multiples was important, but so was gaining experience in getting it right in the first few shots.

Inside the main school's studio area, I was happy with the angle of the sunlight coming through the upper windows. "I think we got the timing right this time," I said to Mark.

"You have more patience than I," he said.

"I hope you're happy with the finished product."

"I'm sure we will be. I'll be showing the progress to the Preserve group soon. Maybe you'd like to be there?"

"Sure, I'd be happy to if the timing works out. Can you email me the information and I will let you know?"

"I'll forward the time and place to you right now." Just as Mark reached into his pocket, his cell phone rang, startling him and almost causing him to drop it. I could only hear one end of the conversation. It wasn't good news.

"I'm at the Hillside. Yes. Then they're on their way?" He hung up, tucked his phone away, and hurriedly put his jacket on.

"Mark, what is it?"

"The tour guide of a group by the tower found what he said could be a dead body. I have to get up there right now."

"I'll come with you, Mark."

We almost crashed into Mandy as she breathlessly entered the school. "I heard screams coming from the tower area. Hurry. Something's horribly wrong."

CHAPTER TWO

Our run up the hill toward the Romeo and Juliet Tower left me gasping for breath. The thought that I had to get myself in better shape was quickly forgotten when I saw a body lying in the tall prairie grasses. I recognized her but couldn't come up with a name. She had recently joined the Historical Society committee.

Mark knew her. "Oh my god. It's Kara! She volunteers at our gift shop."

The tour group had been moved down the hill and out of sight of the body. The guide spoke briefly to a young groundskeeper waiting nearby on an ATV. The man nodded and drove off on the path toward the main house as the guide approached us. "She's that volunteer in the gift shop. Loved hiking the grounds after work hours."

"Andy, have you checked for a pulse?" Mark asked him.

"Not yet," Andy answered. He stepped carefully through the tall grasses surrounding the body and felt the side of her neck. He looked back at us, shaking his head.

"The police and ambulance have been called and are coming in the back gate. I tried to keep the group from trampling around her in case they would destroy evidence. Should I continue the tour?"

"As if nothing happened? I suppose that's the best we can do," Mark said.

A member of the tour group walked up toward us and handed Andy her large fall shawl. "Poor girl. Please cover her with this."

Andy was rattled, uncertain about what to do. He didn't reach for the wrap, so I did. "Thank you. I'll cover her." I took the large orange and brown plaid shawl from the woman's hands.

"She looks so peaceful, doesn't she?"

I smiled and clasped the woman's hand before turning and gently covering Kara's upper torso and head.

"Please let the scarf travel with her when she's picked

up. I have no further need for it," the woman said, before returning to her tour group.

Mark put his arm around Andy's shoulder. "I'm going to talk to the group. Are you okay with continuing the tour for those who want to?"

With a deep gulp, Andy nodded. "Sure boss. If you think that's best."

"I do," Mark said. He walked toward the group, who anxiously waited to see what was going to happen. "I'm Mark Peters. We are all upset and deeply saddened to learn someone has passed away here at Taliesin. It appears she was hiking and simply passed on. Perhaps a heart attack or a stroke. This discovery has certainly disrupted the flow of your tour. I understand most of you have come from other states. Andy has agreed to continue the tour, though in a subdued manner. For those of you who would like to continue this walking portion with Andy, please do so. For those of you who would like to return another day or be taken directly to the main house, please walk back down to the Hillside School, where I will have a shuttle pick you up. You can join a house tour or return to the visitor's center to receive a credit for your ticket."

The group reorganized itself, figuring out what each one wanted to do.

Mandy and I hugged. "Not what I pictured our day going like," I said. "You okay?"

"I will be. But I need to sit down," she said, her fingers interlaced under the round ball of her pregnancy. "Baby Drake did not appreciate the jostling I gave him hurrying up the hill."

Mark walked back up toward me, his sense of strength gone now. He began to speak, but the words caught in his throat. "I just had lunch with her at the visitor center yesterday. She's been a volunteer here for a long time."

"Oh Mark, I'm so sorry for your loss. Poor thing. And so young. I've met her. She's a new member of our Historical Society. Has she been ill?"

"She mentioned that new position and had been talking with our treasurer, Gladys, about bookkeeping for a nonprofit. Sorry, I didn't answer your question about Kara's health. She has a heart condition, but her doctor kept it under control with medication. It involves constant and careful monitoring. Her heart must have stopped working."

"But what was she doing way out here?" I asked. "We're far away from the main house and the visitor center is even further."

"She loved to walk the grounds after she was done in the gift shop. She'd laugh and say that ever since her over-the-hill 40th birthday party she wanted to do everything she could to stay healthy." He slowly shook his head.

"They're here for her now," I said, moving aside.

Paramedics and our Chief of Police Jeff Mathis came walking up the trail through the prairie grasses. Mark introduced himself and told them about Kara Davis.

"Do you have next of kin information?" Jeff asked him.

"I'll go back to the office as soon as we're finished here. Or even better yet, I'll reach out to staff right now and at a minimum get her emergency contact number."

"Thank you. I'd appreciate that," Jeff said. "Well, hello there, Jacqueline Parker. Imagine meeting you at the scene of a crime. Wait. No. Not hard to imagine. I seem to recall a few other times we've met this way."

"Ah yes, we have. But you may be wrong on the crime part. She was being treated for a heart condition," I said.

"So maybe natural causes this time? Still, a dead body and you standing over it, I've seen that before."

Jeff left my side to walk toward the body. He took a branch and moved it carefully through the tall grasses near her. His cursory search of the surrounding area seemed to satisfy him that no obvious clue was there. He waved the two emergency medical technicians in with their stretcher to remove the body.

Across the surrounding hills, deep oranges, rich rusts and vivid yellows dominated the forests, reflected in the shawl draped shape being lifted to the stretcher. A large raven screeched as he flew overhead. Above him, in a perfect V-shaped wedge, Canadian geese flew south to their winter homes.

The EMTs passed by me on the way back to the ambulance with their stretcher. The harsh reality of what was under that shawl snapped me back to the moment.

Jeff pointed toward Mandy. "She okay? She's looking pale."

He was right. She should get back and lie down. "Mandy's due in a few days. I probably should have stopped her coming up the hill with us."

Jeff shrugged. "What are you two doing here, anyway?"

"I'm doing a special photography project for the Taliesin Preservation group, and I needed some better shots inside the Hillside School. The angle of the sun today was going to be perfect. Mark was with us when he got the call."

Mark reached down to give Mandy a hand up. She stood with a wobble, grabbing his shoulder to steady herself as I hurried over. "I'll be fine. Just the quick walk and then seeing her. Felt light-headed there for a few minutes. I'm sorry, but can we leave now, Jackie? I think I should lie down and put my feet up."

"Of course, I think we're done here. Do you need anything else from us, Jeff?"

"No, you take care of that new little life inside of you, Mandy. That is what's important now."

Circle of life, I thought. One has moved on and one is about to make his appearance.

Mark handed his business card to Jeff. "Her husband's name is Nick Davis. This is his cell phone number. He works in Greensville, I believe. I think Kara's parents, the Ericksons, live on a farm along the hiking trail north of town, but I don't have contact information for them."

"Thanks Mark. I'll talk to him and get their number. You go ahead and make sure Mandy gets back to her car. I'll call you later if I need anything. Oh, and do you know who her doctor is?"

"Dr. Dawn Trueblood, right here in Harmony," Mark said.

Jeff nodded. "I'll want to consult with her on that heart condition. In a woman this young, we'd normally do an autopsy. But based on what the doctor says and the family's wishes, things might be different."

CHAPTER THREE

Mandy and I stopped at the visitor center building, which also housed Mark's office. From here I could see the banks of the Wisconsin River. The sandy beaches held the charred remains of beach bonfires from the summer. Now, with cooler temperatures in the air, the beaches were almost empty. An elderly couple walked their two dogs, and a mother, along with her bundled up toddler, sat on a blanket spread across the sand.

"And the world keeps spinning," I said to Mandy. "Are you feeling better? I'll pull up under the front entry canopy and just run in to Mark's office for the marked-up proofs he has for me. You stay in the car. Okay?"

Inside, the news of Kara Davis's death had reached the staff. A cashier at the gift shop looked like she'd been crying. A man behind the ticket window helped those from the group who'd been at the tower. Life went on.

I found my way to Mark's office, next door to his assistant Gladys. She was on the phone telling someone the sad news. I overheard her letting the person know they'd be taking up a collection for funeral flowers.

Mark stood at his desk, rifling through some papers. He uncovered the manila folder he'd been looking for. "Sorry. I'm just off my game. I still can't believe she's gone."

"Was she feeling okay when you had lunch yesterday?" I asked.

"She seemed fine," Mark said. "Gladys was with us, too. We like to treat the volunteers to lunch and make them feel appreciated. Kara was rather quiet during the meal. We chatted about her recent birthday, how busy and successful her husband was, and the fact she'd joined the Historical Society. I think she mentioned something about recent issues with the treasurer there and that she had plans to assume that position. That was about it."

"So, you think she left for her walk after the lunch?"

"No, she had to go back to the gift shop to work a few more hours. We've been shorthanded since the college kids left. She was staying until closing, so probably drove up to the estate after that."

"Again Mark, my deepest sympathies," I said.

As I passed by Gladys's office door, she caught my eye and held up her finger, indicating I should wait. She wrapped up her phone call before coming around her desk to hug me. "I was so sad to hear what you all discovered today. I still can't believe it! She was such a gentle soul."

"Not how any of us expected the morning to go. My condolences to all of you here. I can tell she was well liked."

"Thank you, she certainly was."

The phone began ringing again and Gladys reached for it as I waved goodbye and left.

*A*s soon as we got back to the studio, I sent Mandy home to rest.

"Get the right light for the photographs you needed?" Todd asked.

"I think we did. Our session was cut short, though. The body of one of Taliesin's volunteers was found. It appears she died last night while taking a walk."

"Whoa. What happened to her?"

"Looks like a heart attack or a stroke. She was discovered just lying there, like she'd fallen asleep."

"Did you know her?"

"Not well. She just became a member of our Historical Society committee. Todd, you can leave now if you want. I'm going to work with the photographs from this morning and finish some markups I just got," I said.

"If you're sure. I'd love to take my kayak out while the weather is still holding."

"Absolutely. You have been a life saver, Todd. When you agreed to take the job, I'll bet you never thought you'd be spending so much time in the studio."

"No problem. I enjoy it. Plus, it keeps me in the loop of activity on Main Street."

"Feeling the pulse of Harmony?" I laughed.

"That's right! See you later. Oops, I almost forgot. Libby is still out in back. She was sleeping in the sun, and I didn't have the heart to wake her."

Hannah Sutton passed Todd as he left. Hannah and her husband owned the antiques store across Main Street. She was the chairwoman of our Historical Society and looked upset about something. I wondered if she'd heard about Kara.

"Jackie, I'm sorry if I'm bothering you, but I just had to run this past someone before our next meeting."

"Take a seat. What's troubling you?"

"I'm so angry," Hannah said. "I've been going over the Historical Society books. I agree with Kara's assessment of our money situation. Something smells in Violet's accounting. Stinks in fact! I'm at the point of confronting Violet, but you know how she can fly off the handle."

"I've never witnessed that myself. But Hannah, I have some…"

"I've been trying to reach Kara. The irregularities she pointed out when she reviewed our books are sinking in. I think Violet has been embezzling from us. I've heard rumors that after her husband died, she blew through the life insurance money. You know how she likes to dress and entertain."

Hannah certainly was worked up. I wasn't sure how to tell her about Kara.

"She hasn't returned my calls." Hannah leaned close to me. "I wanted to warn her that Violet found out about the accusations being made against her and believe you me, she does not like it."

"Hannah. Please stop for a minute. I need to tell you something. And after what you just said, I think you should talk to Jeff."

But she was off again. "You're darn right I'll talk to Jeff. I'm ready to bring charges against her. I'm not talking about a small amount of money here. Since we completed the conversion on the house and grounds, our bookkeeping has gotten more complex. And we've had huge increases in our revenues with more tourists and events. Why, I don't know how…"

"Stop. Please. Listen to me. Kara Davis was found dead just a couple of hours ago."

"What? No! That can't be. We just talked on the weekend. I left her a message yesterday," Hannah said. "Where was she found? At home? Or please don't tell me it was a car accident. Nothing violent. She was such a gentle and beautiful woman."

"It was quiet and peaceful. It appears she died last night while she was walking on the grounds of Taliesin. Her body was found by the Romeo and Juliet Windmill Tower this morning."

"Her heart, I bet. Too young. And here I've been rattling on about my own troubles. I can't take this to Jeff now. I'll wait until after the funeral. But I don't know if I can compile the proof I need without her. A forensic accountant, that's it. We should hire one. Poor Nick. And her parents. She was an only child, you know."

"I didn't know that. But why I was suggesting you tell Jeff about Violet was in case it wasn't her heart," I said.

The lightbulb went on in Hannah's mind. Her eyes widened. "You think this might not be her heart? That she might have been murdered?"

"All I'm saying is that Jeff should hear your perspective about Violet's state of mind concerning Kara."

CHAPTER FOUR

The next couple of hours flew by. Time to close the studio, pick up our walking buddy, and hit the trail. The sharp crispness of the air hit as Libby and I stepped out the front door of the studio.

We headed over to the village offices to meet Patti Hunt, our village administrator, ex-wife of Scott, and soon to be grandmother to Mandy's baby. She was joining us for our walk on the Mary-Go- Round Trail. The trail was named after Mary Bell, the wife of a prominent judge, who spearheaded the effort to establish a hiking trail that encircled the village.

Over the past couple of years, many extensions and connections were made to Mary's original trail because of the growth of activity on the northwest corner of town. After Eleanor Harmony donated her family mansion and grounds to the community, the Harmony Museum and Nature Center were created. Fueled by the passion of our Historical Society, the Center saw explosive growth this past year. Events like the Antiques Fair, Blues Festival, and Haunted Hills Halloween drew in hundreds of visitors. Now trails from the Nature Center connected to the Go Round trail. It afforded tourists and locals a path to walk to and from the downtown area or up further into the hills to enjoy even more of the natural beauty of the Driftless area of Wisconsin.

The Hills Resort and Driftless Golf Course, adjacent to the Harmony Nature Center, enjoyed easy access as well. Guests and residents enjoyed using the trail for walking and biking. But they had to leave their golf carts at the trailhead… no motorized vehicles allowed.

Another location with access to the trail was the Harmony Hill Cemetery. I wondered if that was where Kara Davis would be buried.

Patti greeted us. "Hey girl," she said, bending to pat Libby's wiggling body. "Up for a long walk? No running off after squirrels this time though."

"Libby and I have had a serious conversation about that," I said. "She understands but wouldn't give me a guarantee. I think Mandy would like to be walking with us too if she wasn't so pregnant. She's always telling me that Libby needs a refresher on her obedience skills."

"How's Mandy doing? I can't wait to hold my little grandbaby soon," Patti said as we crossed the village green and headed toward the marina.

"Did she tell you what happened to us today?"

"No. Is she okay?"

"She's fine, but we had an unexpected experience this morning and it wore her out. We were at Taliesin when Kara Davis's body was discovered. You've heard about that I assume."

"I did. Such a sad thing. I know her parents well. Their farm is next to my family homestead. When I work in my garden at the farm, her mother Inis often comes over to chat. She taught me so much about gardening and the natural health benefits to fresh organic food. I called her when I heard about Kara. Both Ericksons are very upset. I can't fathom what it must feel like to lose a child. She said they're sure it was her heart."

"She looked like she was sleeping. Just lying there. I've never had children so I can't claim to know what they are feeling. I can only imagine the powerful waves of grief they are experiencing," I said.

"But Jackie, what does this have to do with Mandy?"

"She was with me reshooting the Romeo and Juliet

Tower. Mark Peters, the head of Taliesin was with us. He got the call that a body had been discovered near the tower, which was just above the school grounds where we were. Mandy ran up with us to find out what was going on. It's a sizable incline from the school to the tower. She probably overdid it."

"I'll check in on her later tonight," Patti said. "That whole thing sounds traumatizing, both physically and emotionally. I hope she called Matt. I'm so proud of my son. Watching how he's stepping up and helping. I can tell he's over the moon excited to welcome his own son into the world."

"He is a great husband, Patti. I know Scott is proud of how hard he's working to prove himself."

"Jackie, how are you and Scott doing?"

At this point in my life, I considered myself lucky to have the companionship of such a smart, kind, and incredibly handsome man. It was relaxed. Easy. In the past I was the one who got itchy feet to move out of relationships. This time felt different. "It's good Patti. Really good. We enjoy each other's companionship."

"He's a good man Jackie. I should know," Patti said.

"Do you ever regret divorcing him?"

"I've thought about it so much, but regrets can eat you alive. If I regret anything it was marrying him. It was wrong of me. But then I realize I can't regret marrying him because if I hadn't, I wouldn't have Matt." She shrugged. "You know the story. Scott did such an honorable thing to let me go. I know it hurt him, but he wanted my happiness and knew it wasn't with him. The hurt I caused him is my biggest regret in life."

We walked west out of town toward the Riverview Motel and up into the hills. I unleashed Libby. As soon as she drifted too far into the woods, I called her back and rewarded her with a treat. This dog training is work. I loved seeing her free of her leash and running, but I knew I'd be heartbroken if I lost her. She was my baby.

As we made the turn that took us further up Libby raced down to the very spot Paul Griffin had died. She sniffed and ran. Stopped. Sniffed and circled again.

"Come Libby. Come girl." I clapped my hands and held out the treat. It worked! She came back right away. I never liked this bend in the trail, especially after learning it was being called Deadman's Curve.

When we passed the junction of the nature center trail, I was reminded about the Historical Society link to Kara. "Hannah told me that Kara had uncovered discrepancies with the books of the Historical Society. Lots of money flows through the society's treasury. Especially after the busy summer we had here in Harmony."

"That rumor has been making the rounds. Violet is supposedly denying everything being said about the museum funds. She's loud about it too. Indignant. But she's a strange duck."

The fall colors enveloped us as we continued. Libby was having a blast chasing in and out of the woods. She returned with tiny shards of leaves stuck to her coat. She stopped in the trail ahead of us to do a shake-shake.

We approached the cemetery entrance, and I made Libby stop to take a drink of water from the container I carried in my pack. The side path through the graveyard led down among the headstones and to the street below. In my mind this marked the halfway point of the trail's loop from the marina where we started out.

"Are we good to keep going or do you want to take this cutoff and head back to town?" I asked.

"I think we have enough good light to keep going. I was hoping we might run into Inis and Martin. Their backyard borders the trail, and they often stroll on it this time of day. I feel they need a hug about now. Tomorrow they'll be having to meet with their pastor to make funeral arrangements."

"I'm good with that." I picked up Libby's water, and we were off.

Passing open farm fields, we saw final crops had been harvested, and the fields prepared for the next year's crops. In the distance I caught the lowering sun's rays bouncing off the river.

A couple ahead of us walked hand in hand. He was balding and wore red suspenders over his flannel shirt. The woman's gray cardigan had round patches on the sleeves. Her hair was covered by a small scarf tied under her chin.

"First night without their daughter," Patti whispered. She strode ahead, calling to the woman and extending her arms. They embraced for a moment before she reached for Martin. His weathered farmer's face crumbled as he leaned against her.

I didn't want to invade their private moment of grief. But Libby felt it too and jumped right in the middle of the three of them. She was a wonderful distraction. Inis bent to pet her, and Martin smiled as he wiped his eyes. Patti waved me over. As soon as I got close, she introduced me.

"I can't express how sorry I am for your unbelievable loss. Please accept my deepest sympathies." I almost choked on my words. Here I stood in front of Kara's parents, and I was at a loss for words. I suppose there are no words for moments like this.

"Thank you very much dear. We are still in shock," Inis said.

"Have you seen Nick?" Patti asked.

"We haven't seen him," Martin said. He stood erect, rolling his shoulders back. "But we spoke to him."

Inis touched her husband's arm. "This is a hard time for all of us."

He let out a deep sigh and mumbled. "Sorry."

Patti observed them before she said, "Inis, Martin, what is it? Please tell me. Maybe I can help."

Inis choked back a sob and took Patti's hands. "You and your family have been such good friends over many years. We love you for asking, but this time I'm afraid there's nothing to be done."

"He's cremating her body tomorrow against our wishes," Martin said in a clipped tone.

Inis quickly added, "We don't mind the cremating, though it's not our preference. But we'd like to have a traditional Lutheran wake and service first."

"He's hellbent on getting her in an urn as fast as he can," Martin spit out. "Without a thought to what we might want."

"Now dear. He said this is what Kara wanted."

"Not even doing an autopsy? On a forty-year-old woman? I can't believe that." Martin's face collapsed again. It was hard to watch this powerful man suffer.

"Why not?" Patti asked. "I thought that was automatic."

"We did too. But apparently her doctor would have

done the autopsy, and based on her knowledge of her medical condition she ruled her death a heart attack."

"Dawn Trueblood is her doctor, right?" I asked.

"Right. The family could have requested one be done, but Nick refused to do that. I believe the law makes him the direct next of kin, legally responsible."

Martin clenched his jaw. "So, we just accept it?"

"Yes, I'm afraid so, Martin. At least he's letting her be buried in our family's area of the cemetery where we can visit her. He is pushing the crematory to have the ashes ready so we can have the burial on Friday."

Inis sniffed and took a deep breath. "Well, we'd better turn around and head back home. Our resident herbalist, God bless her heart, has prepared some special tea for us." She took her husband's arm. "It will help us sleep tonight."

We left the Ericksons and continued along the trail on its descent to the edge of the Wisconsin River. Heading west, we passed Harris and Sons Marine Maintenance and saw Shady Pines Retirement Village ahead.

Aunt Ruth and her Shady Pines gals sat on lawn chairs enjoying cocktails and appetizers. They invited us to join them, but the sun was setting, and we had to keep moving. However, Libby was of a different mind knowing she'd get treats from this group. I let them feed her one of the small sausage bites from their spread.

We walked on toward the Stone Mill Brewery where we waved to locals Nadine and DuWayne enjoying a beer on the patio. By the time we hit the stretch of the trail that ran between the village green and the shoreline, the streetlamps were lit.

We parted ways with a hug.

Both Libby and I had a restless night. I pushed myself out of bed, finally accepting the fact that Wednesday was going to happen whether or not we were ready for it.

Since the studio didn't open for hours, I decided to take Libby for another morning outing down Main Street, across the village green, and out to the shores of Lake Harmony.

We weren't the only ones up. The high school cross-country team, on a morning training run before classes started, passed by me. Fishermen were leaving the harbor. Murphy's Coffee Shop was open. Smells of fresh cinnamon rolls drifted out the door and lured me in. After saying good morning to Grace and Dermot and picking up a hot coffee for the walk, we were back on our way toward the marina.

Rocco, having his morning coffee on the deck of his cruiser, waved me over. "Good morning, Jacqueline, just the person I wanted to see."

He was a transplant from Chicago too. He had his boat, the *Roccome Baby*, brought in for the summer season. The boat was named after a song his jazz singing wife loved. Having been a detective and then a private investigator for decades, he too was interested in taking it a little easier at this point in his life.

"Hey Rocco, what's up? You're going to be frozen in place here if you don't put this in storage or cruise back to Illinois. I'll miss having you around. When are you heading to Chicago?"

"That's kind of you to say. I've been stalling taking her back to Lake Michigan. And I am happy to let you know that I recently decided to store her at Harris and Sons. She'll be here all winter and ready to go out on the lake next season."

"Wonderful news! I'm glad to hear that we'll be having you with us next summer. So will you come visit us over the winter?"

"I'll let you in on something else I've been considering. I might try what you are doing. Straddle both worlds. The big city and the small town. I have some feelers out with Kim Walters about finding a nice little apartment here so when I visit, I have my own place. It's been great staying on board the boat, but once it's in storage, I don't think Travis would be happy to see me sleeping on her in his warehouse."

"That's a terrific idea, Rocco! You just made my day. I'm going to Chicago less and less, myself. But my loft is still a good place to keep for now."

"I hear you were there with a very good friend a few weeks ago. Did you have a pleasant time? I don't mean to be indiscreet or appear nosy but if true, I'm happy for you, Jacqueline."

Feeling a flush cross my cheeks, I smiled and said, "All I'll say is yes, it was an enjoyable time."

Rocco said, "Well for what it's worth, I think he is one of the good ones. But you're a big girl and I have a feeling you already know that. Now, what's this I heard about you discovering another body?"

I rolled my eyes. "Is that what you heard?"

"No, just teasing. I'm sorry. I heard that you and Mandy were up at Taliesin when the body was discovered though."

"We were. The woman, Kara Davis, had recently joined the Historical Society, and that's the only way I recognized her. She volunteered at Taliesin. Sad. Looks like natural causes though, not murder this time," I said.

"So not another big murder mystery for you to be thrown in the middle of?" Rocco said with a wink.

"Right. And I'm grateful for that. After that whole 4th of July fiasco, I was glad the rest of the summer was smooth sailing."

"Agreed, that was a complicated, tangled situation. Now, on to what I called you over for. I need to catch you up with how the search is going."

"You've found something more? I was afraid to ask. It's been so long since anyone mentioned it. What news do you have about my half-sister? I should say sister. I've decided that since she exists out there, and I only just found out about her late in my life, I'll skip the half thing. It would be lovely to have someone to call my sister."

"Your aunt and her pals at Shady Pines have been hard at work eliminating possibilities. With a common last name like Smith, it hasn't been easy. She moved from Florida, which you already knew. The gals at Shady Pines found old yearbooks online with photographs of Caroline. I could show them to you but for now let me say that they revealed her participation in the school's theater productions. She seemed to be the star of them. In the 'what do you want to do' section, Caroline said she planned on going to New York and pursuing a career in the theater. It is possible she moved to New York. So that's good news."

"And the bad news?"

"We lost that trail. She could have died, but no death record or obituary was recorded in New York City. She could have married, changed her last name, and lived in Poughkeepsie. The records of that are not easy to find but the gals continue their search. She could have changed her name to a stage name which is not uncommon in the acting profession. She might have gone from Caroline Smith to Petula Pony for all we know. I'm checking out the city theater groups in case she still worked in the field but couldn't make it in the big time."

"That's a lot of could haves." Even I was surprised by the strength of the sigh that escaped from my lips. "What saddens me is that I may never find her. That we will never meet."

"Hey, don't give up hope. It's only been a few months since you even discovered she existed."

"You're right, Rocco."

"Chin up," he said with a smile.

"Thanks for the update on Caroline. Fingers crossed."

· · ·

On my way back to the studio I noticed Stuart Walters inside his office. The Harmony Hills Happenings newspaper was his baby. He'd been a reporter for a larger newspaper conglomerate before buying the failing Harmony paper and returning it to a level of success. The people of Harmony and the surrounding townships looked forward to receiving the physical copy twice a week. Stuart had also built up an online presence for those who accepted that way of getting their news. Local businesses ran low-cost ads in both versions to help support Stuart's efforts in providing our little village with local news, obituaries, sports scores, and special events.

"Jackie, what a wonderful surprise! Come on in. I had a feeling you'd stop in today. Yes, I did." He opened the Murphy donut box next to him on the credenza and triumphantly held up a maple frosted donut.

"You are clairvoyant sir, and I am grateful," I said, reaching for the donut and taking a seat. "What are you working on?"

"The obituary for Kara Davis."

"Don't the funeral homes write those up and send them to you?"

"They do. Inis called me at home last night, all apologetic about disturbing me, but she said she wanted to be sure her daughter's obituary got in the Friday paper. I have received nothing from the funeral home, so I was glad to take in the information she gave me."

"Patti and I saw Inis and Martin Erickson on the trail last night. It seems Kara's husband is directing how the arrangements are going. He's having her cremated in Greensville, so nothing went through our local funeral home."

"Ah, that helps explain things. It surprised me when Inis said that the family invites you to join them for a graveside service on Friday. What surprised me more was that Nick called me when the digital version showed up on the website. He said to change it to a private ceremony. Well, I can tell you I was torn. I mean the guy is her husband, and he was serious."

"Their relationship with Nick is strained. He's trying to do what his wife wanted regarding the cremation, but Inis and Martin are struggling with the fact Nick doesn't want a church service. What did you tell him?"

"I said since the parents gave me the information, I was more comfortable leaving it the way they wanted."

"Good way to settle it."

"But Jackie, something rather startling just happened that makes me question what is going on at a whole different level." Stuart shifted nervously in his desk chair as his fingers drummed on an envelope in front of him.

"Oh really?"

"This was waiting in my mail drop. I'm not sure if I should share, as it was addressed to my wife." Stuart slid the envelope over toward me. "I've never met Nick, but apparently my wife has."

The outside of the envelope had three letters pasted on it…K I m.

"I called her immediately as the paste-on letters were disconcerting. Kim told me to open it. I did."

"Why do you want me to see it?"

"You have good instincts, do you think it's a prank? Be careful, the note inside is a cut-and-paste job too."

I slid my chair closer and leaned forward. With my fingers pinching the edge of the paper, I gently pulled the note out. It read…

CHAPTER SIX

Stuart's uncomfortable reaction was understandable. The cut-and-paste letters created an ominous feeling. The words, *tell the police what u no about nick and ddt,* had a threatening tone to them.

Stuart explained that Kim would be in soon, but she was at a loss as to what the note meant. "She told me Nick Davis owns a title company, so she had interactions with him at real estate closings. But what the ddt refers to..." Stuart shrugged.

"Kim likes to be in the mix of what goes on in the village. As a realtor that makes sense." I tried to frame my next words carefully. "She's also gotten some notoriety for her involvement with the investigations of recent murder cases. Might this be why the note went to her?"

"Excellent point, Jackie. I know my wife can be a touch over the top, but she helped solve those cases, didn't she?" Stuart's eyes narrowed. "That could be it. But if someone was suggesting Kim knew something she should tell the police, why not just send the note to the police? Information could be given anonymously."

"Agreed," I said. "They must think Kim is a unique link to Nick. All that comes to my mind when I see the letters ddt, is that deadly insecticide DDT."

The note puzzled me the rest of the morning. Again, my curiosity got the better of me. Downloading and organizing the Taliesin photos from yesterday was what I went into my computer to do, but I ended up researching DDT. I discovered that the United States banned it as an insecticide because it proved deadly to bird populations and had detrimental effects on some small animals. It is colorless, tasteless and almost odorless, but it is not deadly to humans. Exposure to large amounts would first cause obvious effects like tremors and seizures, long before it would kill a person.

So why bring it up in a note about Kara's death?

When Todd came in at noon, he found me staring at my computer screen.

"You look like you could use a break. At least stand up and stretch. Dolly has her chicken dumpling soup on special. Why don't you go down and have a bowl? That's one thing I love about working here. The chance to get real original comfort food."

"I thought a big city kid like you would want to have comfort food with a twist or the new trendy style of comfort food," I said, with a certain sarcasm in my voice.

"Hey, no picking on this city boy. I loved visiting all the new hot restaurants when they opened, but my mother, and especially my grandmother, made sure I appreciated the traditional food they grew up with. The Glacier's Edge at the Hills Resort has enough trendy offerings for me. Dolly's Diner does the heavy lifting on comfort food. Wildwood provides traditional supper club style, which I was not familiar with, but reminds me of Chicago's great steak houses. Yum! And Stone Mill Brewery does pub fare up right. So, I'm good!"

"Now that you have my mouth watering I will take your suggestion," I said.

"Anything special you want me to do today?" Todd asked.

"If you could unbox the shipment of prints that

arrived from our next exhibitor, that would be great. She emailed regarding pricing and suggested placement. You might go over that and call her if you have questions."

"You got it. Now go enjoy that soup. It's a perfect fall day for it."

Once outside I turned to admire our window display featuring an artist from the Upper Peninsula of Michigan. She'd captured the Lake Superior shoreline during changing seasons. That reminded me I wanted to get a few more fall shots for Wanda's promotional calendar. I'd better move soon on that, before a high wind or hard frost knocked the colors out of the trees.

Val had stepped up her Cut-n-Curl outdoor display a notch. She staged orange and yellow mums around a large bale of straw with a spill of pumpkins and gourds. Inside the salon Val was hard at work. I knocked on the window and waved. Both Val and her client in the chair returned my greeting.

Across the street, Hannah's antique shop window displayed a Halloween theme. Old mannequins were dressed as witches, mummies, and vampires. Maybe they were mannequins left behind by my mother when she closed her dress shop.

The diner was a seat yourself sort of place. I chose a window booth so I could look out toward the village square. Dolly signaled she'd be right over with my coffee.

I noticed Kim leaving Stuart's office. By the expression on her face, I could tell Stuart showed her the note. I quickly texted her to join me. From my vantage point I watched her pick up the text before looking in my direction and giving me a thumbs up. Soon Kim was sliding into the bench across from me.

"You look great, Kim. Love those boots." That perked her up.

"Thanks Jackie," Kim said, extending her foot back out of the booth. She twisted her ankle to admire her boot. "I slipped away on a shopping trip to Madison yesterday. This saddle leather color was just what I was looking for."

"And that sienna cashmere turtleneck. Stunning with your hair color."

She beamed. "You just made my day. Have you ordered? I could use something to eat. Fall weather and soup. Perfect. I know what I'm ordering." Kim slid the menu to the edge of the table. "Stuart didn't even notice my apparel. He was only concerned with making sure I saw that creepy note."

Dolly showed up, coffee pot in hand. "Okay now, what can I get you two fine looking gals?"

"I'll do the chicken dumpling soup. Big bowl, please."

Kim said, "The same."

"You got it. Be right back," Dolly said. "Except you better have a smile when I get back. It's a gorgeous day out there. No frowns."

"Was I frowning?" Kim popped a big wide smile. "Better?"

"Yes, ma'am it is," Dolly said, spinning around.

"Stuart showed you that note, right?" Kim asked.

"He did. We both assumed the Nick it referred to is Nick Davis."

"I guess," Kim said. "But I don't know what it means. But it's plain old weird. Cutting out letters and pasting them on paper. Who does that? So old school."

"Do you know Nick?"

"Sure. He has a big title company in Greensville, and I do business with them. We've been to some of the same conventions over the years. But what that note implied was something nefarious." She leaned in, her eyes bright again. "Could this be a clue? Maybe Kara was murdered! Poisoned with that horrible insecticide. Maybe…"

Kim sat back in her seat as Dolly set our soups down, along with a plastic basket of saltine crackers.

"Talking about Kara?" Dolly asked. "Poor thing. She used to work here. Fact is, she stopped in just a couple days ago. Seemed troubled."

Kim said, "Maybe she wasn't feeling well then already. Like bad things were building up inside her body. Then bam…the poison struck her dead."

Dolly just shook her head at Kim. "You have an active imagination."

"You don't know what just got dropped off at our office. You might not be so dismissive to me. You do know I have a bit of a reputation for a powerful intuitive sense, don't you?" Kim paused, waiting for an affirmation from Dolly as to her supposed skills.

Dolly rolled her eyes. "Right, Kim." She looked at me and said, "Jackie, I have something I want to talk to you about. Will you be here for a while? The noon rush is hitting."

"I'll be here. Stop over and join me when you aren't so busy," I said.

Kim leaned over her coffee cup to squeeze my hand. "Only you, Stuart, and I know what the note said. Do you think we should keep it a secret? Maybe I'm being drawn into another murder case with you. Oh, by the way, how is it you are around when bodies are discovered?"

"Believe me, Kim, it wasn't where I wanted to be."

"And they are sure it was natural causes? Not something more nefarious?"

"Kim, seriously. You almost sound like you'd rather it

was a murder," I said. "By all measures it appears to be natural. Let's eat up. I'm starving."

"Yes. Plus, I have a doctor's appointment to get to. I know I'm going to be puzzling all afternoon about that nasty note. It must have something to do with Kara. The killer might know how I've helped solve cases, and they wanted to give me a clue. Remember when I helped you trick the psychic? Guess her abilities were on the blink. Say, do you know if they ever charged her with Janet's death? I'll bet she set it all up. I was on their boat that night. Remember? And I thought I heard…"

Kim rambled on about the murder cases that had hit Harmony since I moved back. Cases she ended up being involved with one way or another. Directly or peripherally. How Kim managed to finish her soup before me carrying on that rambling conversation I couldn't figure out. But she did it, and left in time for her doctor's appointment, promising she'd catch up with me later.

The lunch crowd cleared out and Dolly had a moment to join me. "You ever get that feeling in your gut that something is just off?" Dolly said as she moved into the seat Kim just left.

"Do you mean like intuition? Sure, I get those feelings."

"I've heard women are more in tune with them than

men," Dolly said. "That's why I wanted to tell you. I figured you'd understand."

"Because I'm a woman?" I asked.

"Yes. And also, you seem so grounded. Gossips or troublemakers might take what I want to say and use it to stir things up. Make themselves feel important. In the know. But you won't. Did you ever hear about the murders that happened at Taliesin in 1914?"

"I didn't. Tell me."

"They happened when the house was being built. Julian Carlton, who worked there, started the place on fire then axed to death seven people, including Mr. Wright's lady and her two children. Some people escaped and put the fire out, but the tragedy was a powerful thing in the community."

"Whoa. That's quite a story. I'm surprised I never heard about it."

"Yes, it was a traumatic event. But the guy who did it must have been a mental case. They never could come up with a different motive." Dolly shifted uncomfortably in her seat. "I got that story stuck in my head last night. Did anyone have a sense about that murderer, Julian, being a loose cannon? Did they think things but not say anything that might have prevented the crime? Then Jackie, sure as you are sitting across from me, I remembered a dream I had the night before last. I dreamed someone dangerous was here again. I tried speaking in my dream. To tell everyone about it. But you know that dream thing where the words don't come out of your mouth?"

"Or you want to shout, and it just comes out like a whisper? I know that feeling too." I almost laughed but Dolly's serious face across from me stopped me.

"That's all. I just had to tell someone. Take a load off my mind." Dolly's fingers moved over the tabletop. Brushing cracker crumbs into a small pile. Sliding an unused knife to one side.

"Dolly, what is it?" I asked.

Dolly didn't look up but said, "Yesterday morning I just figured I had an odd dream. But now I wish I'd said something."

"About what? Did you think the dream was a premonition?"

"Not then, but now I do."

"Are you talking about Kara? Dolly, she had a heart attack. You couldn't have warned her."

Dolly shook her head. "I think there is more to it."

CHAPTER SEVEN

olly is a straight shooter. She doesn't take guff from anyone. I took her words seriously. I'd never seen her so discombobulated. A message in a dream? That just wasn't like her.

Dolly had gone on to talk about Kara stopping in more frequently the past few weeks. Not really saying anything important, but like something was weighing on her mind. She explained it usually happened when the diner was busy, but that she should have parked her butt down next to Kara and made time for her. Dolly was clearly expressing her disappointment in herself for not being there for her friend.

Was she having typical feelings of guilt when someone in our life dies unexpectedly? I supposed she needed to tell her feelings about it to someone who would listen. Like she wished she had listened to her friend Kara. But the dream. Dolly seemed to connect the two things. To me it didn't point to Kara being murdered. Dolly told me about her dreams and feelings. She told someone, me. What should I do with it?

Things were astir. Kim's strange note about Nick. Dolly's concerns about speaking out if we sense something. And to top it off, we had a Historical Society meeting tonight where there was bound to be a confrontation regarding Violet and the accounting issue.

Todd handed me a couple of phone messages as soon as I got back to the studio. "And those came for you," he said, pointing to a fall bouquet from The Flower Girl. The attached note read...*Can't wait for this weekend. Xoxoxo*

"Ohh! Look at all those hugs and kisses," Todd said, peeking over my shoulder. "What's happening this weekend? Must be something special."

I was pleasantly surprised. This was unusual for Scott. He was much more apt to bring in a bouquet of wildflowers for me. "We're having a cookout if the weather holds," I said. "But this reminds me to have Kate deliver an arrangement to the cemetery for Kara's funeral."

I flipped through the messages. The last one was

from Jeff. It took me a few minutes to return the first messages before I could call him back.

"What's up, Jeff?"

"Stuart showed me that goofy pasted up note waiting for Kim at their office this morning and Kim told him she doesn't know what it means. I noticed you having lunch with her when I drove by Dolly's. Did she tell you anything more? Like maybe something she didn't want to share with her husband?"

"No. Nothing. She didn't seem to be hiding anything about it. Just said she didn't get it. Why don't you ask her?"

"I tried, but I got her message machine."

"She had a doctor's appointment after our lunch, so maybe she got hung up there," I suggested. "What did you make of it?"

"Puzzling piece of information. Could it be just some goofball?"

"I assume it has something to do with Kara's death," I said.

"Really? I didn't put that together. Dah Jackie."

"Hey smartie, watch yourself. How does Kay put up with you?"

"Kay appreciates my keen brain and quick wit."

"And how you wear your hair," I teased him.

"She does? That's good news. I'm trying to win the lady over and every little bit helps."

"Now back to the note. Have you questioned Nick? Isn't it always the husband they suspect first?"

"I talked to him yesterday to inform him of his wife's passing. Wasn't an interview though. Didn't see any necessity at the time."

"How'd he sound?"

"Distraught. I followed up with Dr. Trueblood, as she is both the victim's doctor and our medical examiner, to confirm the issues with Kara's heart. Apparently, Nick already communicated with her. They were on the same page about not needing an autopsy. The doctor recently tested Kara's blood to make sure she was on the right balance of her heart medicine. Her blood workup was normal, maybe a little higher than usual, but she said even diet can cause fluctuations. She agreed that all signs in the body pointed to a natural death. Not uncommon for someone with Kara's health issues."

"It seems settled then," I said.

"Question or statement?" Jeff asked.

I knew I couldn't bring Dolly's premonitions in right now. But they remained on my mind. "A little of both I guess."

"You're not telling me something, Jackie," Jeff scolded.

"Patti introduced me to Kara's parents on the Mary-Go-Round Trail last night. They were in a daze, but grateful that at least they would get a burial in the Harmony graveyard where their family is. Apparently, Nick had a contentious relationship with his in-laws. He didn't want any service, period. Just a cremation for now."

"Really? No wake or church service?"

"That is what they said. But he agreed to a small graveside service. In fact, Stuart said that when her parents gave him obituary information, they were inviting people to attend the service and Nick said to change it to a private service."

"My personal opinion, that's cold."

"Stuart thought so too. He left it as her parents requested."

"Good for him. But now this note thing. I might call Nick in to see what he thinks about it."

"I hope you'll talk to Kim first and see if she's thought of anything more. She seems to get things right more often than not, but I've learned she can take a meandering path."

"You're right," Jeff said. "If I can get Kim to focus, maybe it'll make more sense to her. Thanks for your help, Jackie. Are we still on for the cookout at Scott's on Saturday?"

"Far as I know. See you then."

There, messages all taken care of. Now to call Scott and thank him for the flowers. He didn't answer, so I left a message saying "I received a gorgeous bouquet of flowers. I wanted to thank the sender, but the card wasn't signed."

I was texting Kim about meeting me later after the Historical Society meeting. I wanted to go over more of what I had learned about DDT and try to help her focus.

She texted back that she had dinner plans with a client but also wanted to meet later. She had NEWS.

Had to chuckle, Kim was enthusiastic if nothing else. Maybe her NEWS was a clue to what the note meant.

The front door chime sounded as Mandy came into the studio with her cute pregnant waddle.

"Well, hello there," Todd said. "You didn't have to come in today."

"I know. You are a doll to cover for me, but I wanted to get on the office computer and do some work on the photos we took yesterday at Taliesin. It's just easier if I take a little time now while it's fresh in my mind," Mandy said, rubbing her back.

I heard Libby scrambling across the floor at the sound of Mandy's voice. "Hey girl, I heard you behaved on the walk yesterday." A treat appeared out of her pocket and of course Libby sat and waited in perfect form.

"Oh look," Todd said, pointing across the street. "That actress is back in town. She's coming out of Hannah's store, and she has someone with her. An older woman. Do you think that could be her mother?"

We all hurried over to the large display window, but the women were walking away, their backs to us.

Mandy clapped her hands. "This must mean she's going ahead with shooting a movie here! I'll have to ask Hannah more about it tomorrow. They were probably looking at her store again for one of the sites to shoot in."

"I must admit I googled her," Todd said with a little grin.

"I imagine you wouldn't be the only one," I said. "What did you find out?"

"I approached this like I was prepping for a blog post, as I hope to get an actual interview. It turns out I follow her on Facebook and Instagram and those provided the tons of information about Alli Turner. She's had a few small parts as an actress, but her dream is to produce and direct a movie."

"That makes sense," Mandy said. "It seems like that

would describe the scouting of locations that she's been doing here."

Todd rattled off a few facts about Alli. "Her father is a famous director and her mother a soap opera star. They've been divorced for years. She's been in some of her father's movies, but she'd rather be a director like him. The soap opera her mother was in was canceled a few years ago. There's been nothing in Variety about this project though."

"I suppose it takes a long time to pull together all the pieces. Maybe she's trying to keep it under wraps until there is more certainty," Mandy said as she sat in front of the computer. "What's Variety?"

"The go-to for entertainment news," Todd answered. "I keep searching their site every day. I hope I get to meet her in person while she's in town."

"It would be a real boost for the village if it works out," Mandy said. "Okay. Got the uploads done and filed in the project folder."

"What am I going to do without you when the baby comes? Please take as much time as you need," I said. "But hurry back."

Mandy laughed. "Mom is begging me to turn the baby over to her shortly after birth. She is definitely in Grandma mode. But thanks, Jackie, that's good to know.

I'm thinking I can work from home for a while and then come back part-time in a few weeks. See you guys later."

Todd tidied up the shop and left as well. The quiet time with Libby curled up at my feet would be good. I opened the photos Mandy had just filed and pulled out my notes. We'd gotten more shots than I remembered.

These would work well for the past to present transformation technique I planned on using. I would use black and white photos of the school and morph them into these current photographs. We were careful to shoot from the exact angles to make the editing easier. I opened up Mandy's shots outside of the building yesterday. Still so hard to believe there had been a body lying in the tall grasses surrounding the tower.

I noticed she caught some of the tour group as they climbed the hill. I suppose she stopped shooting, as it would involve too much editing to take them out of the photo. I zoomed in and out, making note of some touching up we might want to do. Like taking out the path created for tourists to climb the hill, the directional sign that was near the tower, and the figure standing on the other far side of the hill. I zoomed in. He'd be easy enough to erase. But what was he doing up there to begin with?

I immersed myself in the photographs and almost

lost track of time. I wanted to make tonight's Historical Society meeting and get an idea of where things were headed with Kara gone.

CHAPTER EIGHT

The Harmony Historical Society met faithfully once a month without fail. Even when one of them passed away unexpectedly.

The Society's offices were located atop Harmony Hill in the mansion built by local lumber baron Frederick Harmony, the founder of our village. Once their family home, his granddaughter Eleanor donated it to the community, and they made it into a museum and event center. The Society ran it along with the expanding nature center on the grounds surrounding it.

We were holding our meeting on the second floor in rooms that weren't open for tours. Cookies donated by Murphy's waited in their usual spot on the credenza against the far wall with the coffee urn. After the day I had, I would have preferred something with alcohol in it. But I'd be meeting Kim later for drinks at Shorty's so I figured I could manage until then.

My Aunt Ruth and her friends chatted with Hannah, and I joined them, snagging an oatmeal raisin cookie as I walked past the credenza.

"Jackie," Aunt Ruth exclaimed. "You didn't tell me about Kara!"

"You're right. I'm sorry."

"And you were there when they found the body? My goodness but how does that keep happening. You lived in a big city with all sorts of crime and then you come here and bam. You've seen more crime in a year than probably your entire time in Chicago."

I gave Aunt Ruth a quick hug. "Crazy hah? Though correction on that. This death wasn't a crime. Doctor is ruling it natural causes. Do you want me to move back to Chicago? Maybe the murders will stop."

Ruth gave me an evil side-eye. "Don't you dare, Jacqueline!"

Eunice nudged me. "Don't look now, but Violet is here tonight. Oh boy...fireworks! I can't believe the dingbat showed up after what she did."

She acted like she didn't notice everyone staring at her. Violet held herself in high esteem and was dressed to the nines in a stunning, and costly, Ralph Lauren blazer. I only knew because I had the same one hanging in my Chicago loft. Didn't wear it much these days.

"You mean with the treasury?" I whispered back to Eunice who was gleefully rubbing her hands.

"The embezzlement. The theft. She's going to get her comeuppance."

"I thought it was still under investigation," I said.

"Believe you me she'll want to put the kibosh on anyone looking through the books she cooked. It'll prove she's guilty," Eunice said, with specific emphasis on the word guilty. "And that can't happen in Violet's world."

Violet's gaze snapped toward us, and with a sharp thrust of her chin, she spun away. Eunice acknowledged the action by snickering and giving me an I-told-you-so look.

Hannah gaveled the meeting to order. It took a few minutes for everyone to grab another cup of coffee or bottle of water before taking a seat on one of the chairs lined up alongside two long narrow folding tables that would be taken down and stored away after our meeting. One agenda item that kept being pushed up to another meeting was the purchasing of a permanent conference table. But the thrifty community members could never quite pull the trigger on it when so many other ways to spend our funds were more important to them. I tried imagining the outrage if what Eunice said was true, that Violet had been stealing funds. There goes the conference table purchase.

Hannah immediately addressed Kara's death. She thanked everyone for asking about flowers, but that Kara's parents had reached out and asked that donations be made to Taliesin, a favorite of their daughter. It was quickly decided that we would take a collection. Hannah produced a sympathy card she'd purchased on the coffee table, placing a small box next to it. "Please leave your donations in the box and sign the card. I'll see that Kara's parents get the card with information of our donation. Jackie, would you take the donations to the director at Taliesin?"

"Of course, Hannah," I said.

"With that taken care of, I'd like to open the floor for discussion concerning our now vacant treasurer's position."

Violet stood. "I assumed I would be reappointed."

It was one of those you could have heard a pin drop moments. Uncomfortable coughs and chair shuffles sounded as people turned to look at her.

Hannah didn't mince words. "The committee has concerns about your accounting methods, Violet. I think it best that it be someone else for now. At least until things can be cleared up."

"Let's get this out in the open right now." Violet wasn't cowed by Hannah's remark. She pushed her shoulders back and continued staring at her. "Kara Davis was the person who accused me of overstepping my duties. She was wrong. The books and accounting are correct. She did not complete even one month as treasurer and in that time produced no evidence to justify her suspicions."

Violet stomped her black patent shoe for emphasis. "I won't have my name besmirched without proof or a way to defend myself. I will not stand for it. Slanderous rumors are flying all over Harmony. The village I love."

Dorothy stood. "Hannah, if I may."

Hannah nodded, obviously relieved to turn things over to another committee member.

"I move that we collect any of our records Kara has at her home. After the funeral, of course, but before we nominate a new treasurer. Perhaps we can have every-thing brought here for further forensic examination by someone with extensive accounting experience."

She turned to look directly at Violet. "I personally am sorry if you feel we did not handle this properly, but what was brought to our attention was serious enough to pause your position as treasurer until we could straighten it out."

Eunice cleared her throat, trying to hide the fact that

a laugh was ready to burst out. Betty shyly hid her grin behind her hand. Ruth, however, stood up next to Dorothy and said, "I second Dorothy's motion. And further move that we immediately hire a professional accounting firm."

"And one that is honest and doesn't need money," Eunice whispered.

The color of Violet's face matched her beautifully draped silk scarf. "What was that, Eunice?"

Oh, dangerous move, Violet, I thought as Eunice stood up next to her friends. In an exaggerated voice, speaking very slowly and clearly, she said, "I believe an accounting firm should analyze our books. One that is bonded and professional. They will be paid and there is no danger we will be missing more funds from our bank account when they are done."

Violet flew across the room toward her. "Why you little…" I blocked her dive by grabbing the back of her Lauren blazer and hanging on. Her lovely scarf tangled around her chin, nearly choking her. She only stopped tugging when Hannah pounded her gavel.

"Stop this right now. Everyone calm down."

Eunice's eyes bugged out at Violet, taunting her.

Violet scowled back at her. "That was uncalled for. I demand an apology."

Eunice looked around the room with her now innocent looking eyes. "Whatever for? I said nothing against you. I merely extolled the benefits of using an accounting firm. I never said anything about you, Violet. My, my, we are touchy tonight, aren't we?"

I thought I heard an actual snarl from Violet.

Hannah pounded her gavel again. "Order! Order! Everyone, sit down."

Violet jerked away from my grasp and tugged at her scarf before stomping out of the room, her head held high, her scarf still hanging in a haphazard position over one shoulder.

"How dare she come here and assume she'd get her position back!" Dorothy said to Hannah. "Aren't we on the point of filing charges against her for embezzlement?"

"We're still investigating the matter," Hannah said quietly. "But it will be harder to prove with Kara gone."

Harry Cooper, another Shady Pines resident, said in his usual dry way, "Why should that be? If the books show three plus four equals five, we know something is wrong."

"Harry, you know it's more complex than that," his friend Elmer Fisher scolded. "I second whichever one of you moved to hire an accountant to review what Kara has done and continue on with an investigation. As for

Violet, well she'll just have to step back and wait for the outcome."

"That woman, who just made a scene, will not step back of her own will. She's a troublemaker," Harry said.

"Harry, can I appoint you to bring to the board three possible accountant's names and price breakdowns?" Hannah asked. Before Harry had a chance to answer, she continued, "All those in favor?"

The yeas, including Harry's, were unanimous. The committee moved on to discuss winterizing the recent plumbing at the kiosks on the event field.

When Kim's text came, saying she was at Shorty's, I excused myself and headed back to town.

CHAPTER NINE

Shorty's Bar was an institution in Harmony. It was the place my teenage friends and I first went to see if we could get served beer. Wanda succeeded easily. Val did okay. But me, not so much. I wasn't good at faking it and Shorty could see that. When I moved back to Harmony, it surprised me to see him still tending bar here. Even with the new places that came to town, his business didn't decline. He probably made just enough money to get by, but he always said it kept him going.

Kim waited for me at the bar. She had a white wine. I ordered the same. Apparently, they'd been discussing the possibility of using his bar for a setting in the movie.

Shorty leaned against the scarred wooden surface. "This deal, the movie, is about what again?"

"I'm not sure what it's about except that it must be set in the 1960s. She looked at settings that could be used without too much changing of things. Much of Harmony is stuck in the 60s. Like they are going to use Hannah's store and the Whitlow Bed & Breakfast. Maybe even Val's beauty shop," Kim said.

"I haven't been in the beauty shop lately, but I walk by, and Val's has changed little. She even has some of those old hair dryers my wife used to sit under. The antique store used to be your ma's dress shop, right Jackie?"

"It was. Hannah kept most of the beautiful wooden cabinets, display cases, and woodwork because it fit with her antiques. She said old stuff looked great in an old space."

Shorty just about bust his gut laughing. When he caught his breath and stopped coughing, he said, "That about describes me. Old stuff in an old space. Think I look good?" He fluffed his fringe of gray hair and made a kiss mouth. "Maybe I could even play the bartender. After all, I was here in the 1960s."

"That's the spirit, Shorty. So, can I bring Alli by to see the place then? They'd pay a good price to lease it for the time they need it," Kim said. "Oh, and I have an idea. Maybe they could use you as a consultant. Like to tell them how it looked originally. Or maybe they have staff to do that? Do you ever watch how long the credits are after a movie? I usually don't but Stuart and I had a date night in that new movie complex in Greensville and it was so comfy. Jackie, do you know they have recliner seats there now? Course you would! They probably had them in Chicago before you left. Now where was I?"

Shorty spoke. "You were…"

"Oh, I know. Some of those names on that long scrolling list might be consultants on settings. Stage dressing, is that what they call it? Or is that just for plays? Alli said she doesn't have a huge budget. You could offer to do it for half price. And she said there would be lots of chances for walk-ons. Anyway, Stu and I were so comfy he fell asleep, so I watched the whole lineup of credits and…"

Shorty winked at me, sharing an understanding of Kim's tendencies to randomly weave thoughts together.

"Bring her by. I'd like to meet this gal. Sounds like we could work something out. Now if you'll excuse me, I have customers to take care of."

I grabbed the wine I'd ordered and steered Kim to a booth.

"Sounds like the movie thing is moving forward. We just saw Alli with an older woman. Is that her mother? The one who wrote the memoir?"

Kim adjusted her skirt and crossed her legs. "She is.

They are staying at Kay's B&B again. If you ask me, I think her mother is helping with the money end of things. And probably her dad too. Things in Hollywood are so different from here. Divorces are no big deal, and everyone gets along afterward. In fact, I remember Gwyneth Paltrow didn't divorce, she decoupled."

"We have our own divorced couple who still get along really well."

"True! Your boyfriend and your friend. Scott and Patti. I forget about that. It was so long ago. How's that going for you? He's such a cutie and with that Sam Elliot voice!" Kim touched the tip of her finger on my arm and made a sizzling sound. "Yawsa! He's a hot one."

"I agree with your assessment."

"You are so right, Jackie. He has that cute kind of shyness. Like he's just a little unsettled around women. I know he avoids my innocent flirting. I love teasing him like that. But this lady is happily married to my getting a bit too pudgy Stu."

"Stuart is the best, Kim. You're a lucky lady. But now, what's the news you have?"

"Oh right. I know you saw the note Stuart got. I think I figured out the puzzle of what it means. And the DDT doesn't refer to pesticide."

My ears perked up. "You did? That's great. What does it mean?"

"It happened at the doctor's office. Just my annual physical so normal sort of stuff. They drew my blood to send in for a blood test and that reminded me to ask about Kara Davis. You know she saw Dr. Trueblood just a day before she died. Or two days before. Did they determine the time of death? If it was before midnight..."

"Kim, the news?"

"The doctor said she couldn't talk about other patients, confidentiality and all that stuff. So, I told her I understand. Then I ask about Nick. Did he want to confirm his wife's blood test or talk about the autopsy? How did he seem? Was he really upset? Where was he when she died?"

"Those sound like good questions, Kim," I said, trying to get her out of the loop she was in.

"So now hold on. The doctor said they only had a short phone call so she couldn't tell much about his reactions. I said since you know him, how do you think he's doing? Well, she stiffened up and said she didn't know him. That Kara was her patient, not him. So, I say well I remember back a year when I was at his title company in Greensville, and I saw you come out of his office. And it's like she chills. Collects herself and remembers she used his services for titling a property or something like that. My investigative antenna started humming. She was way too defensive about something. It was such an odd reaction."

"But how did that lead to you figuring out what the note meant?"

"Well, there's one or two more steps in between. I didn't make the final connection just yet. I got dressed and waited in the exam room for Judy, her medical assistant, to come in and do some final telling me this and that stuff. But was I surprised when she says 'I overheard you talking to Dawn about Kara. I think the police should have an outside source verify the blood test results.'"

Kim paused, waiting for my reaction.

I wasn't sure what to make of it. It seemed like a reasonable thing to suggest. "Maybe she meant to do further tests on it for some reason. It doesn't strike me as odd. But you seem to think so. What do you think she was hinting at?"

"I'm not sure, but something's up over there. I mean why does Judy tell me that? I'm on alert now. The receptionist is on the phone, I have to wait to get my bill and make my next appointment. I grab the new People magazine. There was an article about Prince Charles and Kate and the cutest photographs of their little ones. So adorable."

"Kim, back to the story please. Where is this all leading?"

Kim took a sip of wine, licked her lips and continued. "I'm flipping the pages to read more and darn if the final page of their story isn't missing. Of course, I flash to the note. I couldn't figure out just what was missing right on the spot, but I ask the receptionist if she minds if I take the magazine home to finish reading it. She says sure you can take it. We're getting a new one in tomorrow."

"I'm still confused what all this adds up to, Kim. Missing pages out of waiting room magazines might mean there was a good recipe someone wanted or the ad for a face wash. Not necessarily done for nefarious reasons."

"Just wait, there's more."

"Should we get another wine for the rest of the story?"

"No no. I'm almost done. Too much wine makes me sleepy. And I've had a long, long day and want to get home. But this just couldn't wait. I could hardly eat dinner with that client or do any business. My mind was focused on getting this information to you and to help figure out what we can do with it."

I leaned back, guessing I'd have to just let her finish at her own pace.

Kim pulled two People magazines out of her large purse. She held them up. "I took the magazine from her office and luckily the same edition was still in the stores. Now I know what pages are missing. I think we should compare those pages to the letters on the note."

"That's a great way to proceed," I said. "But don't get your hopes up too high. People do that all the time. I know Aunt Ruth used to tear out recipes she wanted to try. She'd justify saying since she had to wait, she figured she'd claim it. If they do prove to be where the cutout letters came from, let Jeff know if you match anything up. At least we'd know the person who sent it was someone who's a patient of the doctor's."

"Wait there's more," Kim said.

Shorty was giving me the cut across the throat movement. "Kim, I think Shorty wants to close up. Can the rest of your story wait?"

Kim said, "No I don't think it can. I know why the note came to me."

"Why, Kim?"

"The sender sent a clue to me not only because of my reputation as a crime solver, but because I know both people it refers to. Nick and DDT."

"DDT is a person? Who?"

"The lightbulb moment came when I got my billing

statement. There at the top of it in a bold classic font, it read from the offices of Dr. Dawn Trueblood, DDT!"

"Wow, Kim. You just gave me serious goosebumps. Are you going to talk to Jeff?"

"You bet I am."

Kim leaned across the table and said, "Might it mean they are having an affair?"

My mouth dropped open. Could it be as simple and as complex as that? An affair? That opens up new ways to look at this. "What even made you think that? Kim, you must go to Jeff with this."

"Jackie, naïve sweet Jackie," Kim said in a sing-song voice. "We may not be a big worldly city, but cheating husbands are everywhere."

And cheating wives, I thought, before quickly pushing my mother's image out of my mind.

"I was planning on telling Jeff today as soon as I walked out of the doctor's office. But then I got busy. Tomorrow morning I'll go to him and put this case on a different track."

"Are you going to the funeral on Friday?"

"I don't think so. I didn't know Kara. Oh, but maybe the killer will be there. They show up at their victim's funerals in lots of the crime shows I watch."

"Kara's death was ruled natural causes. Seems a reach to turn it into a murder case."

Even as those words came out of my mouth, I realized that was the very thing Dolly had hinted at.

CHAPTER TEN

I wanted to catch Mark Peters this morning to go over the progress I'd made yesterday on the Taliesin project. Creating these morphing images would hopefully pull in more views to their website and help promote an understanding of the restoration needs. And that would lead to more donations.

This was a great opportunity for Mandy to work on a project with a bigger scope. She wanted to come along again this morning, and I encouraged that. Working with photographing a subject was one thing, but I wanted to help her learn how to present ideas and deal with the client. But I warned her, no running up hills today!

The photographs we took Tuesday morning were open on my laptop screen and I was explaining to Mark

how I'd digitally taken out things that served no function but would only distract, like signs or that random
figure who photo bombed Mandy's shot.

Mark complimented us on the thorough job we'd
been doing.

We went to the interior shots of the Hillside school
we had and juxtaposed them with old photographs from
its original use as a progressive learning environment
for young students, to the time Mr. Wright transitioned
it to an architectural school.

"You did an amazing job capturing the morning light
on these," Mark said. "And the angle will work for the
transition from this black-and-white photograph to
now. Well done, Jackie. I'm so pleased with how this is
progressing. We will be able to showcase the completed
restoration work and enhance the fundraising efforts
for further work. There is still so much more to do.
Some days it feels endless. But this project is energizing
me. Thanks to both of you for all your work."

"Thank you for the positive words. I'm glad you like
what we have done so far."

"I understand Kara's burial is scheduled for
tomorrow afternoon?" Mark said.

"It is. Are you planning on attending?" I asked.

"I am, along with some of the other staff, especially
the girls in the gift shop. That's where Kara was most

well known. Mandy, do you save the original copies of your photographs? Not just these edited ones?"

"We do," Mandy said. "It is easy now with digital photography."

"Can I see the originals of the tower photos?"

"Sure," she said, going into a different computer file. Soon thumbnails of the photographs showed up on the computer screen.

"What is it you wanted to see, Mark?"

"What you took outside. Particularly the figure you mentioned being on the hill."

Then it hit me. Mandy had been photographing the tower just before the body was discovered. I knew what Mark was thinking as I zoomed in on the person standing to the side of the tower.

Mandy realized it too. "I took those just before the tour group started walking up the hill."

"And just before the body was discovered." Mark leaned in for a better look.

"Do you know him?" I asked.

"I do. It's one of our staff. But I don't understand what he was doing up there at that time of day. He's a recent hire. A groundskeeper. We needed more hands to do the fall cleanup, and he seemed perfect. Quiet. Perhaps a little socially uncomfortable. Kept to himself as far as I knew. But I remember the head groundskeeper saying he would be focusing on the property around the house this week. Based on that conversation it's odd this man would be at the tower."

"Maybe he should be questioned?" When Mark gave me a surprised look I said, "Not to implicate him. But if he roams the grounds, he might have seen something. Or picked something up thinking it was trash when it might be a clue."

"Clue to what, Jackie? I understood this was an open and shut natural cause death."

"Me too," Mandy said. "Jackie, are you telling us it's not?"

I'd surprised myself by what I'd said. Did I think her death could have been on purpose? I knew Jeff was keeping the note out of the public so I couldn't mention that. But Mandy and Mark were waiting for an answer.

"Guess it's just the amateur sleuth I've found myself becoming since I moved back to Harmony."

Mark laughed. "No worries. I agree with you about talking with him. He might have seen something. I'll have a chat with him, and you're welcome to let the chief know about this. Do they have a time of death?"

"Hmm, good question. I'll ask him. Time we head back to town now, though. Glad you like our work so far."

As we left Mark's office, I poked my head into the one next door where his assistant Gladys was working.

"Hi Jackie, how are you doing?"

"Great. I might need your help with something," I said.

"Sure, what can I do for you?"

"It's about the Historical Society. I understand you were helping Kara sort through the financial records. Now that she's gone, the committee would like to continue her investigation. Would you be willing to share what you know about her work to date?"

"Absolutely. Please give them my contact information. I will say, the bits she showed me pointed to potentially serious issues."

"How serious?"

Gladys paused and glanced at Mandy. I could tell she wasn't comfortable saying more in front of her. Mandy got the hint too.

"Excuse me, I'm going to say hi to a friend of mine who's working in the gift shop," Mandy said.

As soon as I shut the door Gladys spoke. "Very serious, Jackie. Kara had a mind for numbers. The things she uncovered in the short time she had the books pointed to much deeper and insidious mishandling of the accounts."

"So not purposeful? Maybe Violet just didn't understand what she was doing? That she got in over her head? Especially this past year. The place is so busy. Lots of things were done to get it ready to open. They were very busy handling revenues from the events."

"What I saw were not innocent mistakes. She did it on purpose and cleverly. I don't want to see Violet get in trouble, but she knew what she was doing."

"I understand, Gladys. And thank you for being willing to help the forensic accountants we'll be hiring."

"If you're hiring professionals, they might not need my help. I've got a feeling she was fooling the committee members, but it will be obvious to trained accountants. I'll help where I can."

"Someone will be in touch with you. I'd better get going now. See you at the funeral on Friday?"

"I'll be there. But Jackie, just a moment more. I couldn't help but overhear what you were discussing with Mark. About that man he saw in the photos. His name is Sid Hobbs. Mark was kind in saying he's socially awkward. I have an uneasy feeling around him. I wanted you to be aware of it. And to hear he was up there that morning is surprising. I remember his boss calling me on Tuesday asking if I had heard from Sid. That he hadn't shown up in the north flower beds where they were to be working."

"Was he just late at that point?" I asked.

Gladys shrugged. "He didn't come back at any point that day. I'm telling you this because I want someone else to be aware of it."

What Gladys said sounded familiar to Dolly's remarks about speaking up.

"So, you're saying he was on top of the hill, but then didn't go to work afterward. That is strange. We don't even know if he saw the body when he was standing there. Did he know Kara?"

"He did. I think he liked her. She was nice to him."

"Maybe he didn't go to work because of what he saw. That it upset him too much."

Gladys stood up from her desk and took a deep breath before speaking. "I'm not saying this lightly because I don't know Sid well. But I knew Kara. She complained about Sid's attention making her uncomfortable. That he didn't get normal social cues. In one conversation with me she even used the word stalking."

CHAPTER ELEVEN

By the time we left Taliesin I knew I wanted to touch base with Jeff again. Had Kim gotten to tell him about what she'd told me last night? Could she be right about Dawn being the person the note referred to? And if she was, what did it mean?

The first thing I wanted him to be aware of was that Gladys confirmed the suspicions of the Historical Society committee. Their concerns about Violet's book-keeping were justified. I needed him to hear about Violet's behavior at the meeting. Maybe it was simply Eunice's behavior that provoked her angry lunge and this whole thing might have nothing to do with Kara's death. But it could turn into a crime in and of itself.

Next was the groundskeeper. Learning who that figure in the photograph was, and what subsequently happened, could be important. It might be easily explained, but it seemed worth looking into.

None of my concerns pointed to Kara's death being murder, by any stretch of the imagination. But I'd let Jeff decide what, if anything he wanted to investigate further.

I dropped Mandy at the studio and parked my car. The walk to the station would help me put my thoughts in order.

Our police station was quiet as most small-town ones are. No strange crackling chatter coming across radios. No handcuffed suspects waiting in hard plastic chairs. No stern desk sergeant fielding calls and reporters. Just Patrick Murphy sitting at the front desk.

"Hey Murph. Is Jeff around?"

"Jackie, hi! Nope. He went over to Doc Trueblood's office."

"About the notes and Kim's discovery?"

"You know about that? We're trying to keep it quiet," Murph said. "Pretty crazy though, huh? Good thinking on Kim's part. They compared the note's letters with what would have been on the missing pages. It proved to be the page the letters were cut from."

"Wow, that's quite a discovery. Let him know I stopped in and have him give me a call."

"Will do. Have a good day."

I left the station glad that Jeff was taking Kim's suggestion seriously. I wondered if he would show Dawn the note or just ask her a few questions.

I walked the long way back to the studio and saw Jeff's cruiser outside of the one-story medical building that contained, among other medical professionals, Dr. Dawn Trueblood's offices. Jeff was just about to pull away when I flagged him down. He pulled up next to me and rolled down his window.

"Fancy meeting you here," Jeff said.

"You're just the man I was looking for."

"I won't tell Scott that," Jeff answered.

"I'm not stalking you, Officer," I teased right back. "I looked for you at the station and Murph said you were here. I heard that Kim's magazine investigation proved fruitful. Did you learn anything at Dawn's office?"

Jeff filled me in. "It was hard to explain my questions regarding magazine pages being torn out. I didn't want to bring the note out just yet. I tried dancing around the reason I was there, but it was a losing effort. Dawn gave me the weirdest looks. Finally, I explained someone had pasted together a note from pages of a magazine found in her office. And that the note referred to DDT. Could they mean Dr. Dawn Trueblood? Dawn seemed shaken by what I was telling her."

"It would be a weird coincidence. The note. Her initials."

"She had no idea what the note meant. Claimed she barely knew Nick. I asked if she had anything to share about Kara or Nick. Not necessarily with her death, but maybe a business problem or something along those lines. She thought for a bit and explained how she was limited in what she could say because of client patient privilege, even after death. She hesitated when I said I'd like to talk to her staff as well. Seemed to feel they'd have nothing to contribute. She asked me who received the note."

"Did you tell her it was Kim?"

"No, I didn't."

"Did Kim mention Nick and Dawn knowing each other? That she saw them together?"

"Kim told me that. Dawn mentioned knowing Nick professionally, but not personally, so she covered herself on having been seen with him at his office."

"And the staff? Did they have anything to add?" I asked.

"Now there it got a little hinky. The receptionist couldn't think of anyone who seemed suspicious. So again, I decided to reveal the note's cut-out letters and what it said. Both women were shook up when they saw it. The receptionist still couldn't come up with any ideas, but the medical assistant, Judy, asked me if she could talk to me privately after hours. So maybe she'll know something more. I'm going to meet her later today.

"Jeff, she also remarked to Kim that Kara's blood test results should be reevaluated. It struck me as odd because labs are so accurate. All I could think was that she was implying something wasn't on the up and up. I have a couple of things I came across. I want to dump them into your lap and off my mind. Not sure if they are important to this situation but I'll let you decide that."

"Jackie, jump in. I'm going in your direction. Hannah wants to talk about the Historical Society's accounting issues. Sounds like it got pretty ugly last night. Was that one of the important things you wanted to talk about?"

"It was. Pretty crazy scene. Eunice didn't help by teasing Violet."

"Ah yes, sweet Eunice."

"Today I was at Taliesin to meet with Mark. His assistant Gladys had been helping Kara with the books. She's familiar with not-for-profit accounting practices. She seemed to feel that what Kara was discovering was going to lead to serious trouble for Violet."

"Hmm, she did? Interesting. I figure I'll let our district attorney file charges against the woman if it comes to that. I don't understand why Hannah wants to talk to me about it."

Knowing Hannah has asked to talk to Jeff, she must think the same thing as me about Violet's possible involvement with Kara's death.

"Did you question Nick about the note?"

"He came in without question late yesterday and appeared truly stunned by the note. I didn't sense a guilty look or body language when I asked him what he thought it might mean. He asked me who the note was sent to, but I declined to answer him. We went over what he'd shown me previously, including the text messages he and his wife exchanged on the night of her death. The messages said she had lunch with a gift shop friend and was going to walk with her tonight. But the friend had a change of plans. He said she should keep an eye out for that creep who was bothering her. He texted her that he was going to get a hotel for the night because the drive home was too long, and he was wiped out."

"Who was the creep, as he called him?"

"I asked him that very question. Nick told me there was this guy who worked at Taliesin that Kara talked to occasionally. But then he started bothering her. So that's why he started calling him the creep. He didn't seem overly concerned about the guy."

"So those texts gave Nick an alibi for that night," I said.

"I suppose. But I still don't know why he would need

one. Dr. Dawn was still adamant that it was natural causes."

"Gladys at Taliesin mentioned something to me about that man too. The guy she was talking about showed up in photographs Mandy took the morning they found the body. Strange he'd be standing there up at the tower and then not go into work that day. Gladys said his mother called him in sick."

"This person creeping Kara out saw the body that morning? It could be an innocent reaction. Maybe he was so upset he couldn't work afterward."

"My first thought. But then why would he have even been up there? He wasn't supposed to be working in that area."

"Do you have his name?"

"Sid Hobbs."

Inside Sutton's antiques we went to the back office with Hannah. She confirmed the threatening nature of last night as I had experienced it. She added that Kara felt fearful of Violet. "She's a powerful woman in this town. And now hearing about our committee moving forward with going through the books, I'm sure Violet felt things are heading in a terrible direction for her. Any offer to make restitution is out the door at this point."

"It could mean jail time then?" Jeff asked.

"Yes, it certainly could."

"Are you insinuating what I think you are?" Jeff asked. "Could she have done something to Kara? I mean the doctor says it was natural causes. And she did an external exam and found nothing suspicious."

"I'm only telling you what my takeaways are from last night," Hannah said. "I felt the need to let you know as there might be more than money at stake."

Jeff and I exchanged knowing looks. He was the first to speak.

"Are you thinking what I'm thinking?"

"I'm thinking there's more to her death than we've been led to believe."

CHAPTER TWELVE

A woman I barely knew found dead. Natural causes, they all said. Then clues began challenging that assumption. The note started it. It implied this wasn't as we all thought. A husband who might have had an affair. A vindictive volunteer who didn't want to be held up as an embezzler. An odd man who might be a dangerous stalker.

The why's and how's of Kara's death needed to be explored.

The why's were clear in each situation. Death instead of divorce. Death instead of jail. Death instead of being rejected. All plausible. All possible. But highly unlikely.

Natural causes could still be the answer. But so could suffocation, poisoning, or a hidden reason buried in a hurried cremation.

Did a wacky person with nothing better to do stir things up with that note? Just like in some murder mystery TV show? Odd how it went to the woman who would put a spin on it. Kim loved helping to solve mysteries. I had to stop myself from going down the path that Kim might have set this up for attention. Good grief, Jackie. Stop it!

I pushed open the front door of my studio to find Patti standing behind Mandy, rubbing her shoulders as she took deep breaths while Libby lay across her feet to comfort her.

"What's going on? Is she in labor?"

"I think they are just Braxton Hicks contractions," Patti said, reaching around to hug her daughter-in-law. "Feel better now?"

"Thanks so much, I do," Mandy answered as she patted Libby. "Okay girl, I'm good now. Thanks for cuddling up to me."

Libby wagged her tail before running to greet me. "Hey girl. You making our soon-to-be momma feel better?"

Mandy stretched. "My doctor mentioned these might occur, but it still caught me by surprise."

"Be sure to keep drinking lots of water. Dehydration can cause them," Patti said. "I can't explain how excited I am for my grandbaby to get here. And I know Scott is as well. We'll finally be grandparents! Mandy's parents know what it feels like. How many grandchildren do they have?"

Mandy laughed. "Three. But as my mom says, each one is a fresh new blessing. I'm so happy ours will have cousins to play with. Their youngest grandchild is two years old, so that's close in age. Plus, my friends are having babies now so there will be lots of little playmates in his life."

"Have you picked a name yet?" Patti asked.

"No. I know you are waiting with bated breath, but no final decision. We have a short list of family names we're considering. It might come down to the first minute we look into his eyes. A name might come to us. One that feels right. It won't be Matt. No junior for your son, Patti. I liked the idea, but Matt said it's too confusing. I'll give you one hint though, we might use Scott for a middle name."

"That sounds like my son. His father said the same thing when we were picking Matt's name out. No juniors."

I felt a twinge of jealousy. Patti and Scott would always have this connection. They had a son together. And now will experience being new grandparents. Something I will never have. A ripple of regret washed over me. But choices were made, and I made mine. I'm not good with regrets. They take too many good vibes away, I always say. I loved where my life choices took me. And that now they brought me here, back in Harmony, which feels perfect for this time in my life.

"Did you tell Jeff about that man in the photos?" Mandy asked.

I hated spreading too many stories around town, but Patti looked expectantly at me. I had to think she'd be the right person to talk with Kara's parents when the funeral was over. She could ask if Kara had mentioned someone stalking her.

"Mandy was telling me about him. It seems pretty concerning, don't you agree, Jackie?" Patti said.

Mandy excused herself. "Bathroom calls to me yet again."

"She's such a sweet girl and will make a great mom. I know I'll miss her around here," I said.

"Now just to get her to relax and not stress too much. The baby is due soon and I hope everything goes smoothly. But you didn't answer my question. What is up with your concerns about the man in the photos? Is he involved with Kara's death? Mandy said he worked at Taliesin."

Patti's attention was pulled away by her cell phone ringing. "Excuse me. It's Kara's mom. I should take her call." She stepped out to the front sidewalk with her phone to her ear.

I busied myself going through end of day closing chores. With summer over we'd shortened our studio hours. I reconsidered that decision as promotions by the Hills Resort and the nature center were bringing in so many tourists for the fall colors.

Mandy came out of the back-office area. "Patti might be right about dehydration. I go to the bathroom so often that the water bill here is going to be huge. I might be skipping liquids thinking it'll mean one less bath-room trip."

I laughed at the look on Mandy's face. "I'll finish closing here. You get yourself home and put your feet up. You know you can stay home if this is all too much."

"I'm glad to have somewhere to go. I'd go stir crazy if I just sat at home waiting for the little munchkin to arrive," Mandy said. "But I will take you up on that offer to leave a few minutes early. Matt is taking me out tonight and I wouldn't mind freshening up a little."

"Where are you two headed?"

"To the Wildwood. We're going to get lobster! Treat ourselves before our baby boy arrives and we can't afford it. This outing is sponsored by a gift certificate we got at the baby shower. The card said the parents need gifts too!"

"That afternoon shower was so fun. I enjoyed meeting your family."

"And thank you again for your generosity, Jackie. You didn't have to do that. We put the crib and dresser on the list because we thought family members might go together and get it."

"Sweetie, it was my pleasure. I only hope I didn't take it away from others who wanted to do it."

"Not at all, Jackie. With the opportunity you're giving me to develop and grow a career, my family considers you part of ours."

"I love that! That's so sweet. So, I'll get invited to baby's birthday parties?"

"Absolutely. At least until he only wants to invite friends," Mandy said with a knowing smile. "I remember my first kids only party. I want him to have as great of a childhood as I did. I assume you're going to the funeral."

"I'm planning on it," I said. "Now off with you."

Patti gave Mandy a quick hug on her way out. "Jackie, can you come with me? Something's happened at the Erickson farm. Inis and Martin have gotten a note about Kara."

"A note?"

CHAPTER THIRTEEN

I shut down the register and turned out the lights before Patti and I left for the Erickson's farm in my SUV. On the ride, I explained what I'd learned about the man in Mandy's photograph, and I told her about the note Kim received.

"Kim received that note yesterday morning, and now another was delivered today. What on earth is going on?" Patti said. "Does Jeff have any idea who sent the note?"

"No. When we see the note Inis and Martin have, maybe it'll help. I've seen the first note so I might be able to tell if the same person did it."

The wind picked up, sending leaves spinning. Dark clouds pushed across the sky in the last light of day. The desolate empty fields passed by as we drove to the farm.

Pulling into the yard, I saw dim lights in the windows of the brick farmhouse. Inis greeted us at the back stoop, her gray hair whipping around her head by a sudden gust of wind. Her apron snapped against her.

"Come in. Get out of this nasty weather," she said, hanging on to the screen door so it wouldn't bang against the frame.

Martin sat at the kitchen table, his hands resting on either side of a piece of paper. He glanced up at us. I couldn't discern if his expression was one of anger or disgust. Inis invited Patti and I to sit in the two remaining seats at the table, before she scurried to pick up the supper plates and pile them into the sink.

"This was in with today's mail," Martin said, sliding the paper across to Patti. "I just opened it after dinner."

He stood and left the room. Inis's worried eyes followed him. Patti and I were surprised at his departure.

"You must understand that he needs to get away from this. He is trying to remain in control, but it's been a rough couple of days. He'll be in the barn trying to work out his anger on some chore or outside chopping wood. It's always been like that with him," Inis said.

I leaned over to read.

· · ·

NoTNAtUraL

Patti was just as startled as I.

Inis busied herself with tidying the kitchen as if a note saying someone killed her daughter didn't drop into her life today.

"Inis, please sit down. We need to talk," Patti said.

"I'm afraid if I sit down, I won't get up again. I have to keep moving or I'll go crazy," she whispered.

Patti went to her and took her by the shoulders. "You won't go crazy. We're here to help you."

"Since Wednesday Martin and I have been managing. We met with our pastor. We drank the chamomile tea and took long walks. Collected ourselves. Now this. I don't know if I can hold it in anymore."

With Patti's gentle guidance Inis sat down at the table, averting her eyes from the note.

"Martin was as angry as I've ever seen him. Who did this? Who brought this to us on the eve of the burial of our only child? Who would be so cruel?"

She looked back and forth between Patti and I with questioning eyes. "Does this mean she was killed? That it wasn't her heart?"

"I don't know, Inis. But we need this note to go to the

police. They'll know what to do with it. If you have the envelope, we'll take that as well."

"You should put it in a bag. If someone left prints, they could be picked up," I said.

"From an envelope?" Inis asked with a hint of hopefulness. "Patti, there are zip-lock bags in that second drawer."

"He might catch the nasty person who left this in your mailbox," Patti said, taking a paper towel to stow the note and envelope in a plastic bag she'd pulled out.

After carefully sealing the top of the bag, Patti continued. "Jackie and I will be sure this gets to the police."

Inis pushed herself up from the table and went to the window. Holding the white ruffled curtain to one side, she said, "He's out there in the dark. I can see his silhouette by the fence. Martin feels so helpless. We could live with knowing her heart failed, but now this…"

She took a deep breath, and without taking her eyes off Martin's shadowy figure, she said, "Okay let's talk before he comes back in."

"First, Inis, do you know anyone who might have wanted to hurt Kara?" I asked.

"In the past hour since we opened this, I've tried to think about who might have put this together. Who could be so mean? This couldn't be true. But then after staring at it, we both thought, what if it was…"

She turned toward us. "Could it be true? Kara murdered? You two must think so because you asked if I knew anyone who would want to hurt her."

"Inis, you need to know that there was another note yesterday. The possibility exists that someone is just playing a cruel joke. There is also the possibility that someone meant her harm," I said.

"And the person who left this note might know something but is afraid to come forward," Patti said. "The other note also suggested something nefarious. That's why we need to know if anyone meant her harm. It would give the police a starting point."

"But they've cremated the body," Inis sobbed. "Nick was so quick to insist on that. When Martin read this, the first word out of his mouth was Nick. He only tolerated him because Kara loved him."

"Beyond Nick, is there anyone else?" I asked.

Inis stared down at the table, her fingers wringing the edge of her apron. "I can't think. She pulled out in front of a car the other day and the driver honked at her and shook his fist."

"Who was that?" Patti asked.

Inis looked frustrated. "I don't know. Some guy. I'm

just trying to do what you asked. To think of anyone upset with Kara."

"It didn't turn into road rage?" I asked.

"Road rage? I don't even know what that means."

"Did the guy get out and threaten her?" I asked.

"No. He just drove off," Inis said. "Please, I just can't think. I'm so sorry. I'm no help at all."

Patti said, "Nonsense Inis. You can't create a person out of thin air. Your daughter didn't have enemies. That's a good thing."

"Hold on. This isn't like an enemy, but Kara talked about a guy at work making her nervous. Like he seemed to lurk, hoping to run into her."

Patti and I exchanged glances. The man on the hill in Mandy's photograph. Sid at Taliesin.

"That's the sort of thing to mention," Patti said. "Did she say anything more about him?"

"I don't remember. Wait. She said that she had been nice to him when no one else was. Kara was such a sweet person. Always watching out to not hurt people's feelings. To be kind. But then she said he acted different. It made her nervous."

"Anyone else come to mind?" I asked.

"This seems so out there, but she had been telling me that since she accepted a treasurer position with that historical group, the woman she took over from wasn't happy about it. I hate to suggest any of these would be people who would want to see her dead. I just can't fathom that."

"Of course, you're not accusing anyone directly. But this is the way police and detectives investigate things."

"I can't think of anyone else. Everyone loved her. She worked with the volunteers at Taliesin, and we got a lovely card from them. When Mark, her boss, stopped in earlier today he told us how much she was loved and will be missed. Such a kind man."

"Thank you for sharing that with us," I said. "He is a gracious person."

"I just don't know how we'll get through tomorrow thinking about her being killed. The doctor said it could have been a sudden cardiac event. That her numbers were fine on her last visit. None of us know when God will call us up, but to think someone could have taken Kara's life. It just takes our breath away." Her hands flew to her face to muffle the sob that shook her.

"Maybe we should let you and Martin have some time alone now," Patti said.

Inis reached for Patti's hand. "No, please stay just a minute longer. I don't want to be alone."

"Maybe you'd like a tea," Patti suggested.

"Yes. That would be good." Inis pushed away from

the table and ran her hands down her apron. "I'll make us a tea. Judy brought a new blend with her today."

Patti stood. "You sit, Inis. I know how to work a stove and a tea kettle. I'll brew the tea. Should I use the bags on the counter? That's so thoughtful of your friend to bring this."

"The ones for us are still in the little paper bag. She used the root of a valerian plant which should help us sleep. She's such a sweetheart. Though I wish she hadn't brought in the mail for us."

"Why's that?" I asked.

"We might have not seen that awful note until after the funeral. But now we have. So that's that."

Patti busied herself with the tea. Soon the sharp whistle of the tea pot pierced the air.

A sad smile rose on Inis's lips. "Judy recently brought tea for Kara too. She remarked that Kara seemed stressed, so she formulated a natural tea for her as well."

"See Inis, Kara was loved by so many," I said. "Did the tea help Kara?"

Inis let out a soft laugh. "Not so much. She complained it was too bitter. I teased her and said to add sugar. That some things are bitter medicine but help a person. She kidded me right back. Too much of a good thing can be bad for you too, Mom. And she rattled off the potential side effects of added sugar like high blood pressure."

"Remember the Mary Poppins song about a spoonful of sugar helps the medicine go down. Did Kara have issues with diabetes?" Patti asked.

"Oh no. We were just teasing back and forth," Inis said with the hint of a smile at the memory. "She was very careful with her health. Went by the rules and kept a watch on her medicines. She was comfortable with the tea because Judy works at Dr. Trueblood's office, so she understood Kara's heart health issues."

"That's good," Patti said as she set down the tea in front of us. "I hope this tea doesn't make us sleepy! We have to drive home yet."

"It's delicious. To think this was recently dried. I'm not a big tea drinker, but this might make me consider it," I said. "I'd love to have the one she gave to relieve Kara's stress. My friend could use some stress relief."

"You can have it all. Look for the tag marked with a K." Inis smiled. "Thank you for staying with me here for a few minutes longer. It helped calm me. Knowing that note is getting to the chief brings me some comfort."

"Good. Maybe you'll sleep better. It'll be a long day tomorrow," Patti said. "I suppose we should be moving on now too."

"You'll be coming to the funeral tomorrow?"

"I will," Patti said.

"And you?" Inis asked.

I nodded. "Certainly. I only knew your daughter a brief time, but I want to pay my respects as well."

"The church ladies are putting on a light lunch afterward. Nick controlled so much of this process thus far, but that is one thing he can't say no to. If he doesn't want to join us, so be it. This may be one of the last times we see him. He is already planning to sell the house and move somewhere to open another title company office."

"Maybe that's for the better if things were strained between him and Martin," Patti said.

"I want to share something more with you before Martin comes in. He is upset enough with Nick without hearing this," Inis said.

We all heard Martin's heavy footsteps on the back stoop.

Inis leaned across the table and quickly said, "Kara thought Nick took out a life insurance policy on her last month. The doctor had to do an exam to certify her health."

Whoa, the classic motive for murder, I thought as Martin walked into the kitchen. Wonder what she said about Kara's heart condition in that certification. Might be good to check out.

The morning of the burial of the Erickson's daughter was blustery. Not like the past days where the chill of autumn was welcome because it brought the amazing colors of the leaves turning and those familiar wood-burning smells. No, today's fall weather was bitterly dreary. Funeral appropriate I thought.

I bundled up in my classic camel hair double-breasted coat. I had it over thirty years, and it has never gone out of style. With a gray and camel plaid scarf tucked in around my neck I was ready. The wind gusted between the houses as I made my way to the cemetery. Kay must have lit the wood-burning fireplace at the Whitlow Bed and Breakfast. That odor always meant fall for me, and I enjoyed the comforting smell as I continued on my way.

Several dozen cars were parked on the street leading to the cemetery. I supposed most of those attending came from the country around the Erickson's farm and would have driven in. Kim slipped in next to me and took my elbow as I entered under the arched entryway.

Kim had also chosen a warm calf length coat, but in a deep rich hunter green color that complimented her rich chestnut hair.

"Kim, what on earth is with those sunglasses? You don't need them today with this cloud cover," I said.

She grabbed at her wide brimmed felt hat as a particularly sharp gust of wind threatened to take it. "I need the glasses so people can't see I'm scanning the crowd, discreetly observing the attendees. I'm hoping to see body language from a guilty person."

She demonstrated her scanning abilities, but by turning her head. I didn't have the heart to tell her it would be obvious what she was doing. They didn't need to see her eyes.

"Any clue as to who sent you the note?"

"No. It's frustrating. Hey look, there's Jeff. He's doing the same thing as me," Kim said. "We investigators think alike."

Nick was here as well, standing to one side talking with an older couple. Kara's parents, dressed in their Sunday best, were near their pastor. I noticed Patti join them. A simple urn sat on a small, draped altar. Several floral bouquets and arrangements were clustered nearby.

"Too bad the husband didn't let them have a service in the church. I can't figure it out. What would have been the big deal? What was his hurry? You can see where my thoughts are leading me." Kim pulled her oversize sunglasses down. "I don't believe it. Dr. Trueblood is walking up to the parents. The nerve of her!"

"What's the problem with that? I'm sure she wants to extend her sympathies."

Kim pushed her sunglasses back into place and sniffed. "She's the one having the affair with Nick."

"Kim. Shhh. That's just speculation on your part," I scolded.

"I have a brain, Jackie. Remember, I'm one of the few people in town who has a connection with both of them. Nick and Dawn. That's why I got the note, remember. Someone knew about the affair but couldn't tell. They must have some risk. Or they sent me the note knowing I would tenaciously follow the clues to expose the truth behind her death."

I pulled Kim further away from the people walking

past us. "Kim, someone might hear you. You wanted to be discreet. Remember?"

That admonition at least lowered her voice. "Don't you see? Nick wanted Kara out of the way so he could leave town and continue the relationship. Or at least get out from the taint that will hang over him. Did I tell you he already listed his house with me? I could barely stand to sit across the table from him to sign the papers. But I did it. All the while knowing he was planning to flee this area. Probably Madison, he said. Madison is practically a suburb of Harmony." She paused with a pinched mouth. "Or would that be the other way around? We are almost a suburb of Madison?"

I took my chance to talk. "Madison is well over an hour away. But none of that proves he was having an affair with the doctor. I hope you're not spreading that around town."

"Me? Of course not. I'm keeping this tight to the vest for the moment."

"Except for discussing it in front of dozens of people," I mumbled. "Did you share your suspicions with Jeff?"

"I did, but I don't think he believed me. Not yet. A woman knows these things. Besides when I'm in her office, you know she's my doctor too, right?" Without giving me a chance to answer, Kim continued. "I hear and sense all sorts of undercurrents. Like the thing with the note originating there. Her staff knew I was on to something. Maybe one of them wrote the note to get the affair out in the open. Jeff hasn't questioned them yet has he? Or did he? Why should he? He doesn't have the intuition I do." She tapped herself on the side of the head.

I hoped it would knock some sense into her. She couldn't keep assuming Mark was having an affair, much less with our town's doctor.

"I'm going to work my way a little closer to the action, Jackie. Maybe no one will notice me, and I can do a little eavesdropping."

No one notice her? Fat chance of that. With those glasses and that hat who wouldn't notice her?

Several rows of folding chairs had been set up near the small altar. The Shady Pines group filled six of them. My Aunt Ruth, Dorothy, Eunice, Betty, Elmer, and Harry. They were all on the Historical Society committee also, but it still surprised me to see them out on a chilly day like this. Then I remembered how they enjoyed attending any social gathering. I suppose this ceremony and the luncheon afterward fell into that category. I took a seat next to them.

"Good morning, ladies and gentlemen," I said. "May I join you?"

"Of course, Jackie. We were wondering if you'd show up," Aunt Ruth said, shuffling everyone down a seat. "I heard Mandy had some contractions yesterday. Is she okay?"

"She is. Patti talked her through it."

"Braxton Hicks, right?" Eunice said. "Gets them worked up every time."

Dorothy peered around Ruth to see me. "We've been hearing that Jeff is investigating Kara's death. That this might not be a death by natural causes."

"He is, but he's trying to keep it on the quiet side."

Elmer, who was sitting in the row behind us, leaned forward to speak. "Very troubling to see Violet act so aggressively. We've been talking about it since the meeting on Wednesday. What did you make of that scene she put on? She was mad enough to kill."

"Elmer!" I chastised him. This was getting out of hand. "I talked to Gladys at Taliesin. She's familiar with non-profit accounting and had been advising Kara. Has anyone on the committee reached out to her yet?"

"I think she talked to Hannah," Ruth offered. "These past months the Harmony Museum and Nature Center has seen an enormous increase in the money we handle. Of course, funds flow in and out. But after so many unusual transactions, I'm so grateful the committee is hiring a forensic consultant to comb through records."

"I hope Jeff checks Violet out," Dorothy said. "I could tell him a thing or two about her. And I'm not prone to gossip, as you know. Please let him know that when you see him, Jackie."

I was surprised by what Dorothy said. But to be honest the thought of Violet being involved with Kara's death had crossed my mind too.

"Thanks, I will."

Dawn walked away from the Ericksons, and I caught her looking at Nick. He didn't notice. He was busy choosing a seat in the front row of chairs. Dawn straightened her shoulders and drifted off to one side near us, stopping under a large oak tree. I motioned to her that we could make room, but she smiled and shook her head no.

Mark and Gladys joined the edge of the crowd. I supposed they would step away when the service was done. Beyond them I noticed a woman visiting a grave. She wore a long navy coat with a tartan plaid shawl across her shoulders. Her gloved hand rested against the headstone. Her head bowed. I couldn't make out the name of the headstone, but it was one of the larger ones here.

My eyes drifted back across the cemetery. I thought of the wide spectrum of those buried here. From the large stone the woman was standing by to the modest one with Inis and Martin's names and dates of birth already carved in it. It looked like they planned on burying Kara's urn next to their own plots.

Kara's parents moved to sit at the opposite end of the front row. As far from Nick as they could. Patti sat next to them. The pastor lightly coughed, signaling he was about to begin his service. Single sheets were being passed out. Two prayers and the words of a hymn were printed on them. I was about to walk one over to Dawn when I noticed she'd slipped away.

It was a simple and modest ceremony befitting the local Lutheran farmers. After the last prayer, Pastor John asked for a moment of silence for each of us to remember Kara Erickson Davis.

After a few seconds of silence, a loud gurgling cry startled everyone. It came from a huge raven perched atop the bare branches of a white birch, its iridescent black feathers shining against the gray sky.

The pastor raised his head and said, "Guess he didn't hear my request for a moment of silence!" Which elicited a low chuckle from his audience. "The family has asked me to extend an invitation for those in attendance to join them at St. Paul's Lutheran church for a light lunch and fellowship."

The raven spread his wings, flying across the crowd, over the trees, and out of sight.

CHAPTER FIFTEEN

Those gathered dispersed. Moving along behind them were the men from the church, taking down the folding chairs which would have to be transported to the church basement for the luncheon setup.

"Did you walk over? We could give you a ride to the church," Harry said.

"No thanks, but I'll see you there. Save me a seat!"

Patti was holding Inis's arm as they placed the urn in the ground and Martin began covering it with dirt. The pastor stood with them, his hands clasping his Bible. A private moment I didn't want to intrude on.

Kim waved me over. "You going to the funeral lunch?"

"I am. Decided I'd walk over. Want to go with me?"

"I'll walk you part way, but I can't stay for the lunch. I have to get back to the office."

"Did anything of interest present itself to you at the service?"

"Nothing new. Now I'm convinced Dawn and Nick are lovers. I saw her trying to catch the cheating bum's eye. I think it surprised him she showed up. It was pretty brazen of her."

"Not if she isn't having an affair with him. It might look odd in a small town if she didn't show up. Especially losing such a young patient."

Kim and I began walking out of the cemetery. The path ran near the large monument where I'd seen the woman. The impressive stone belonged to Judge Josiah Bell and his wife Mary. I couldn't help but think about how our lives were intimately intertwined.

Kim and I left under the archway and walked down to Oak Street where we turned to head to the church. Pointing to a late model sedan driving by, Kim exclaimed, "Look, look. It's Alli Turner and her mother. More and more I'm believing that we will have a Hollywood movie made here. I'll have to get a gown for the premiere. I'm thinking a rich sapphire blue. Alli told me I'd look great in that. What color will you get? Something classy and elegant, I'm sure."

"Take it easy, Kim. We're a long way from buying

dresses for a premiere. Are the Turners in town for a while? I know Aunt Ruth would love to meet her."

Kay came running out the front door waving, a tartan plaid shawl draped over her arm. But she was too late, the car's occupants didn't see her.

"You just missed them," Kim said.

"Darn. It's chilly today and Beverly left her shawl."

"Are they leaving town?" I asked. The shawl Kay held looked familiar and then I realized this Beverly must have been the woman at the Bell's headstone.

"No, they are just going to Madison for the day," Kay said. "Are you two coming from the funeral? I'm sorry I missed it. It was just that the timing didn't work with me serving breakfast and guests checking out."

"It was a simple ceremony," I said. "I'm going to the luncheon in the church basement. Kim has to head back to the office."

"I heard I missed a rambunctious Historical Society meeting last night. Not quite what one would expect to happen in such a sedate crowd. Whatever are they going to do with that mess of bookkeeping?"

"Good question. The vote was to have an outside forensic accountant handle it."

"Wow, that's news. Is it really that bad?" Kay asked. "What did Violet do when she heard that vote?"

"She stormed out before it," I said.

"She will be hot when she finds out. She always held herself up as so high and mighty. Maybe she messed up, but she doesn't strike me as the type to say sorry, I made some mistakes. She'd be too embarrassed to fess up right away and get it over with."

"It's not looking like that," I said. "Kara consulted with the person who does the Taliesin foundation's books. I talked to her, and she said any missteps they uncovered appeared serious and intentional."

"Do you both think this Violet person would have wanted Kara out of the picture?" Kim asked.

"I'm sure she did. She made it clear on Wednesday night that she was angry about being slandered, as she called it. Her reputation sullied," I said.

"But enough to murder her?" Kim asked.

Kay gasped. "Kim, you're taking this too far. Kara died of natural causes."

Kim and I exchanged glances that Kay noticed. "Ladies, what are you keeping from me? Out with it."

"Well," Kim said. "That might be the cause of her death and it might not. But we'll talk later, got to get to the office. Coming with, Jackie?"

Kay grabbed for my arm. "What is going on? Jackie, talk to me."

"I'll tell you about it later. Or better yet, ask Jeff. He's up on most of it," I said.

"He hasn't said a word about an investigation into Kara's death. I'm seeing him at dinner tonight, so I'll get it out of him," she said with a wink.

Kim and I continued west on Oak Street. We passed my old home. Such great memories there. Maybe someday I'll knock on the front door and invite myself in. A man clipped shrubs outside the lovely home next door, which had been split into first and second floor living quarters.

"Morning Mr. Harper," Kim said. "How do your gardens grow?"

"Why if it isn't Kim Walters, my very favorite real estate agent. How are you doing?"

"Great. And this is my friend Jacqueline Parker, photographer extraordinaire! You work too hard tending these gardens, Lon. I pop fall mums in my planters and voila, flowers again. Isn't it all over now after that hard frost last week?"

"Now Kim, part of gardening is tending to the fall cleanup. Trimming back bushes, cleaning up dead leaves. All to prepare for the next growing season. Besides, I love doing this. I feel like I'm tucking in my babies for the coming winter weather."

"And we all enjoy the fruits of your labors on display here," Kim said. "How's Kate doing?"

"She's good. Business was excellent this year."

I finally put two and two together. "Are you Kate's dad?"

"I am, and proud of it," he said with a smile.

"She does such a great job with her Flower Girl florist shop. We just came from a funeral and saw her arrangements there. Did she learn about it from you?" I asked.

"I like to think so," Lon said. "She always was the one who liked getting her fingers in the dirt with me. But I can't claim I taught her anything about creating bouquets and flower arches and all that fancy stuff she does. That's all her."

"There's still so much green for this late in the year," Kim said. "Jackie, look at that garden back there. I thought you were more of a flower guy."

"I set that up for my tenant. She has a green thumb too. She even got my old foxglove to have a second fall flowering. Those are mostly herbs back there. She's careful about covering things on the nights we have frost warnings so that helps." He looked up at the sky. "Feels like tonight's temperatures are going to dip way down."

Kim shivered. "And not come back until spring. Well, we're off, nice to see you again."

"Nice to meet you, Mr. Harper," I said as we turned to walk away.

"Please call me Lon. Kim, I'll be reaching out to you. I must list the apartment again. My tenant just gave me notice this morning. Said her son will be taking a job in another city and she'd rather stay close to him. I'll be needing another renter."

"Will do. I'll call you and we can talk details later."

CHAPTER SIXTEEN

t the next crosswalk, Kim turned south toward Main Street. I continued on to St. Paul's Lutheran Church. Its automated outside lights had turned on as the day continued to darken with a thick cloud cover. People entered through a door that led to the basement where the luncheon was being held.

Sounds of clattering dishes and cheerful chatter came to me as I took the concrete steps down. The low ceiling created a warm and cozy atmosphere. The air in here smelled delicious. The Lutheran Women's Club had served hundreds of family style luncheons over the years. Platters of deep-fried chicken were being placed in front of the guests. Dolly's special warm German potato salad, colorful honeyed carrots, and warm biscuits from Murphy's Bakery already sat in large bowls on the tables. Vivid yellow and orange silk fall foliage stems were tucked into simple glass vases that probably dated back to the fifties. These vases held seasonal flowers for countless funerals, weddings, baby showers, and church picnics.

The Shady Pines gang had taken over a table and I headed in their direction but was stopped by Patti. "Jackie, I got the note to Jeff this morning before the funeral. I saw him watching the people coming and going. Did he say anything to you?"

"No, I didn't get to talk to him. How are Inis and Martin doing?"

Patti shrugged. "Best as they can. All this activity is a great distraction. They appreciated you coming with me last night and they asked me to thank you for any help you can provide."

"I'll let you know if I hear anything. I know Jeff will want to talk with the Ericksons when things settle down."

"They want to talk to him but need to get through this day first. One foot in front of the other is how Inis described it. No one else knows about the note they received yet. They'd like to keep it that way until they can talk with Jeff."

"I understand," I said.

I picked up a coffee from the large urn on my way to

the table where a second platter of chicken had arrived. I found myself super hungry. Maybe it was the comfort food I saw in front of me. Or the familiar faces at the table. Everyone was busy taking a helping and passing the bowls and platters around. Small plastic glasses for water sat at every place setting. Paper placemats were printed with ads for local businesses. The members of the Lutheran Women's Club bustled around the basement in their aprons and soft-soled shoes.

"Wasn't that raven call a hoot?" Eunice asked. "The bird of death. How appropriate at a funeral."

Harry said, "In several symbolism references, ravens are deemed to be psychopomps."

"What in heaven's name is that?" Eunice asked.

"Just what I was going to ask," Betty said. "When my great-aunt Constance was dying, she lived with my family toward the end. An old maid, so no children to care for her. She kind of scared me, sitting there with those boney fingers folded on her lap or worse yet when I'd sometimes see her lying down with her eyes sunken and mouth half open."

"Betty, focus. What about her?" Dorothy snapped.

"Oh yes, well when she was with us, I vividly remember blackbirds flying around every day. Or were they crows? Or maybe ravens like you said Eunice. Anyway, big black feathered birds that frightened me."

"If they were big, probably not blackbirds. Now as to the difference between crows and ravens, the easiest way to tell them apart is by their calls. Crows caw, ravens croak," Harry said, reaching across in front of me for the fresh rolls. "Their tail feathers also are different, but that might be too much information."

Dorothy rolled her eyes.

"And you never told us what psychopoops are," Eunice grumbled.

"Psychopomps," Harry patiently repeated the word. "The word comes from Greek mythology. They are creatures who help the deceased cross over to the afterlife. Like a connection between this world and the next."

I shivered, thinking about seeing a big raven the day Kara's body was discovered. There is often truth in symbolism that continues across eons of time.

Betty pinched her lips. "I don't know if we should talk about mythology in a Lutheran Church basement. They might consider it disrespectful."

"Are you saying that ugly black thing was picking out someone else to take on over to the other side?" Eunice groused. "Or was he still working on Kara? Harry, sometimes I can't figure where in tarnation you get things from."

Harry mumbled. "If you'd read once in a while you'd know."

Aunt Ruth just smiled and shook her head. "Harry, we appreciate your knowledge about birds. Which type of blackbird did you say was at the cemetery today?"

His mouth now full of a warm biscuit, Harry raised his finger in a just-a-minute gesture.

But Elmer filled the void. "Raven. Definitely. It was a raven. Solidarity. Crows move in packs. Say did you notice the woman by the Bell family headstone? That family monument looms above everything."

"I did," I said. "And I found out she was the mother of the young actress who's been here in town looking for sites for filming a movie."

Aunt Ruth tilted her head with a quizzical look. "She was by the Bell headstone?" I noticed Ruth's eyebrows drawn together. She picked at her carrots a moment before saying, "I've wanted to meet her ever since I learned she was in Times of Our Life, my favorite soap opera. Guess I'll have to do a stake out to catch her."

"Maybe Kay could arrange it," Betty said. "Isn't she staying at her B&B? It's so exciting that we might have a big movie filmed right here in Harmony."

"Kim's already picking out her gown for the premiere," I said.

Eunice almost choked on what she was eating. "I can believe that. And what color will it be?"

I laughed. "She's thinking a sapphire blue. But I

shouldn't tease. She could be right. Somehow I'm picturing a small budget independent film that might open in Greensville."

"When you lived in Chicago did you see movies being made?" Dorothy asked.

"Sure. Plus, lots of TV shows shoot there too. I had friends who leased their houses for scenes. It's quite a production. They rearrange things, sometimes even paint the walls and change the carpet in the rooms."

"For a TV show?" Aunt Ruth asked. "I loved the sets on that soap opera. I even decorated my apartment in those colors."

I made a vow to connect with this actress and surprise Aunt Ruth. I understood the famous or even semi-famous wanting their privacy being respected. But if the filming happened, it would be good to have a base of people you knew in town too.

Sharp clear dings of silverware against a glass got everyone's attention. Martin stood looking out across the gathered friends and family. "Inis and I thank you all for joining us today and the Lutheran Women's Club for putting on this luncheon. We lost our dear daughter and have been taking it one step at a time to get through the past days. Today, with Pastor John's support and the love we feel from all of you, we are ready to face what happened head on. And to find the person who is responsible for our daughter's death."

You could have heard the proverbial pin drop. No need now to keep the note under wraps I thought. The room buzzed with indistinct murmurs.

Martin raised his hand. "Please, everyone let me explain. We have received a very disturbing note that has forced us to consider the possibility Kara could have been taken from us, not by God's hand, but by the hand of someone among us. If you know of anything that might add to Police Chief Jeff Mathis's investigation, reach out to him."

He paused, taking in the familiar faces of family and friends, before bowing his head. "And God help the person who sent us that note if they did it maliciously."

CHAPTER SEVENTEEN

I had to get to Jeff. He needed to know what Martin just announced. Now it would be common knowledge he was investigating a murder and no way could it be kept quiet.

"Are you kidding me? Way to open a can of worms. Patti only brought their note to me this morning. I'd been planning on talking with them later today," Jeff said.

"You think he was wrong to tell everyone about Kara's death being a potential murder?"

"He had a right to do it, but it makes my job harder," Jeff said.

"He's furious with his son-in-law. If Martin knew about the first note he might do something he'd regret. Or if the gossip points to Dawn as having an affair with

Nick, and all the while being his wife's doctor…I can't imagine," I said. "That's why I wanted you to know about this immediately."

"We need to go warn Dawn and Nick. Or were they at the luncheon to hear Martin's announcement?"

"No, neither of them was there. I don't think that an affair connection is widely thought of. It was Kim's suggestion that it's part of this story. I don't see it myself."

"Kim has some good instincts. It won't hurt for us to talk to Dawn again. Things could get ugly for her if this affair thing is true."

"Who's this us?"

Jeff ran his fingers through his longer than regulation hair in a nervous gesture. I know Kay loved that he wore it that way and I understood why. He was a handsome man with a good heart.

"I thought it would be a good idea if you came with me. No pressure, but you might have a womanly instinct as to the truth of what Dawn will tell me."

"So, now you're thinking I have good instincts?" I teased.

Jeff laughed. "Of course, but the key thing is you don't rattle on like Kim does and end up pouring out too much information. You are more discreet. And you follow a logical path approach too. Kim's random zigzag path sometimes puts her at the right outcome, but, well you know what I mean."

"When you, or we, go to talk to Dawn, should we tell her what was in each note?"

"She knows what's in the first one."

"That's right. I agree. She needs to be pressed. If this second note about causes is true, her career could be in jeopardy. Was it malpractice or coverup?"

"Good point. I think we need to put everything out on the table to both her and Nick. If only the mysterious person who's making these notes would come forward. Or contact me anonymously so I could talk to him. Understand what he knows that we don't."

"At the end of Martin's speech, he threatened the person better not have written the notes just to stir up trouble. The sense of his anger was palpable when he said it. Do you think that's even in the realm of possibility?"

"There are some whackos out there. Even possible that the first note was legit and the second one a copy-cat," Jeff said.

There was no one in the waiting room when we arrived at the doctor's office. The receptionist looked startled to see the police walk in again, but she recovered when Jeff said it was just to clarify a couple of points with the doctor.

"Do you have to talk to me or Judy again?" she asked.

Jeff hesitated a moment. "I have a question about the blood tests so if Judy could give me a couple of minutes, she might be able to answer those."

"They are both with a patient now. Please have a seat. It shouldn't be long."

Judy rounded the corner from the back exam rooms, surprised to see us there. She handed a paper to the receptionist asking her to file it, before turning to us. "What can I do for you?"

"Is there somewhere we can talk in private?" Jeff asked.

Judy ushered us into an empty exam room. "I'm sorry I never got back to you," she said. "It's all just so very confusing."

"Do you have something you want to share now?"

"I don't want to see Doctor Dawn get in trouble," Judy said.

"I understand that. It's best if you tell us. It might be important, or it might not. We need any information you have to help me with this situation," Jeff said.

She looked down at the floor. "I may have misinterpreted."

"How about you tell me, and I'll decide about its

validity?" Jeff's efforts of drawing information out of her were failing.

"Would you like me to leave?" I asked.

Judy's eyes flicked between me and Jeff.

"Look, I promise I'll come in after work today. I'm just so uncomfortable talking here."

"I'm good with that," Jeff said.

"Good with what?" Dawn asked. "I didn't mean to interrupt, but I was told you wanted to speak to me."

She looked at the three of us and sensed the tension in the room. But Jeff managed a quick response. "Good with waiting until you can join us for a couple of questions."

"Well then I'm glad I have a few minutes. What were your questions, Jeff?"

"I don't understand the complexity of Kara's heart condition. But you said her last test results were negative, correct? That means that she didn't have a problem?"

"I guess you could say that. She didn't have a problem with her digitalis levels. These tests are routinely and continuously done on patients like Kara. The balance can easily be thrown off. If it gets out of whack there are serious results."

"I'd say this was a serious result," Jeff said. "Death."

"That can happen even when a patient is being

treated with digoxin. Sadly, it's not unusual, just rarer in someone of her age and health. She'd recently been noting more shortness of breath which would show levels of digoxin were low, but our most recent test showed they were fine. Even a touch high."

Jeff nodded. "Am I missing something? Are digitalis and digoxin the same thing?"

"Yes, basically they are. The body handles them differently, but digitalis is a natural product of many common flowers. It's been used since the 1700s. Nowadays digoxin is extracted from the leaves in a more sophisticated way. I could go on and on, as I find these topics so fascinating."

"Like the history of current medicines?" I said.

"Yes. How our ancestors developed methods to treat ailments. And how the first medicines and healers gained their knowledge. Did you hear of Dr. Beaumont on Mackinac Island who studied the digestive system through an open stomach wound in a patient? Fascinating story. But I digress. What other questions did you have?"

"I can see why you are a good doctor. You want to understand the background and the science behind what you do. But the testing of Kara's blood was sent out of your office for analysis. Could the most recent test results have been wrong?"

"I'm careful to work with reputable laboratories, so I wouldn't expect that. We also monitor potassium and kidney function. It all seemed normal. Nothing to show digoxin toxicity. I did a blood draw when I examined her body. If you'd like, I could have Judy send that to the laboratory for retesting."

"I wasn't aware you'd done that. Is that normal procedure?" Jeff asked.

"No, but I wanted it as part of a research project being done on patients who use the drug. Kara signed papers to be part of that study which included a post-mortem blood draw. I haven't yet forwarded it to the university."

"Yes, I'd appreciate learning about those test results when you receive them," Jeff said.

"Judy," Dawn said. "Remind me to get those to the lab. I'll review the agreement Kara made to be certain I don't need the family's permission for that."

"Will do," Judy said, fidgeting with a box of latex gloves. "If you don't have more questions for me, I'd like to leave now. I think that was our last patient."

"Sure, Judy. Sorry to keep you," Jeff said.

"We're done for the day," Dawn said. "Have a wonderful weekend, Judy."

"You too." Judy looked grateful to be leaving the small room.

Maybe now Jeff could get around to asking Dawn more pointed questions.

Dawn leveled her eyes at Jeff. "I'm sensing there is something more in your questioning than the history of digitalis."

Jeff nodded. "Dawn, I'm going to share some disturbing information with you, and I'll need to ask you a couple of questions about it."

"Sure, go ahead Jeff."

"Where were you the night Kara died?"

His direct question shocked me. Guess that's the reaction Jeff was hoping for from Dawn too. He handed her a photocopy of the note that Kim found and the one left with Inis and Martin yesterday. Dawn took the two papers from him and skimmed what was written on them.

"This first one is a copy of the note I mentioned to you. The second is one the Ericksons received last night. Can you enlighten us as to what these point to?"

She finally looked up. "Why did you just ask me for an alibi on the night Kara died?"

"It was suggested that DDT is not referring to a pesticide, but to initials. For instance, Doctor Dawn Trueblood."

"Jeff, do I need a lawyer?" Dawn said with an uncomfortable laugh. "These are some ludicrous suggestions you're implying."

Jeff shrugged. "I'm fine if you want a lawyer, but I'm not accusing you of anything. I feel compelled to check out the possibility that Kara may not have died of natural causes."

"I'm shocked by the insinuation that I would have any reason to wish or be involved with the death of a patient. For god's sake Jeff, my life revolves around the Hippocratic Oath I swore to when I became a doctor."

"Dawn, I'm aware of that. But it shouldn't be so hard to just tell me what you were doing on Monday night. The night before Kara's body was discovered."

"I was with Nick Davis."

CHAPTER EIGHTEEN

awn's confession about her being with Nick that night opened up a flood gate. She said, "He'll be furious with me that I told you about our affair. I no longer care. I'm tired of the lies and the sneaking around. Something had to give. I was as shocked as anyone when Kara's body was discovered."

"Did you suspect Nick might have something to do with it?" I asked.

Dawn jerked back. "No! Absolutely not." She seemed to search for words. "She died of natural causes. I signed her death certificate."

"With this additional note and your revelation, I'll want to take control of the blood sample taken from her body to hold as evidence," Jeff said.

"Evidence? Of what? Her numbers wouldn't have

dropped in such a short time. It was just for the trial, for the..."

Jeff interrupted her. "I'd also like a contact person regarding those trials."

"What are you suggesting, Jeff?" Dawn could barely get the words out. Her shoulders slumped as the realization sunk in. With no response from Jeff, Dawn said, "I'll ask Judy to get you that contact number. The blood sample is in a transport cooler. This way."

After Dawn gave us the cooler holding the latest sample of Kara's blood, we left.

"Guess you didn't need me to sense what Dawn might say or how she'd react. She just put it all out there. And Kim was right about them having an affair. You could have fooled me on that one."

"We can't check for smothering or strangling now as the body is gone," Jeff said. "Could the marks have been there, and Dawn hid that fact? What a mess."

"The only real chance of proving a potential murder is with the idea that someone poisoned her. That last blood draw might have evidence of that," I said.

"I'm planning on having it tested for common poisons."

"Excellent idea. At least it's something to go on. What about her reaction? She seemed to be shocked that we might think it was Nick."

"And then that led her to realize she could be a suspect too," Jeff said. "Using that famous intuition women claim to have, was she part of it or not?"

"Don't know about the value of my intuition. After all, I missed on the affair that Kim figured out."

"True," Jeff said. "I'm sensing guilt. Dawn covered herself by giving me the symptom of shortness of breath which would indicate heart failure. But then covered with noting the levels of Kara's medication were a touch high which would point to toxicity. Seemed pretty contradictory to me."

"Well now, Jeff, you've been doing some research, haven't you?"

"Just doing my job, ma'am," Jeff said with a grin and a thumbs up. "It was my cousin Wanda who informed me about it years ago. Her husband had a heart condition too and was on digitalis. She was well versed in the symptoms and how hard it was to control."

"Well good for you. Did you ever get hold of the man at Taliesin who was making Kara feel uncomfortable?"

"I called the number I got from Gladys. A woman answered. She assured me she'd have him contact me. But I haven't heard back yet."

"Well, if you want to talk to him, I'd do it soon."

"Why the hurry?"

"I learned he still hasn't returned to work at Taliesin.

And that woman who answered is his mother. She's saying he won't be back."

"Thanks for the heads up. I'll call the phone number again. Was he at the funeral by any chance?"

"I didn't see him there," I said.

"Honestly my focus right now is on Nick and Dawn. Means and motive. The affair and wanting the wife out of the way. Sure is reason enough in my mind. But Dawn didn't hesitate to throw Nick under the bus just now. This is going to be tough. I don't understand how the cremation happened so fast, but I checked with Charlie Hunt, and he said it was legal. That makes her look like either the culprit or a co-conspirator."

"Forgot to tell you that Kara's parents thought Nick took out a life insurance policy on Kara recently."

"Well now, that about seals it. I'll confirm that with them as soon as I can."

"Did Nick give you an alibi for that night? And explain why he wasn't concerned about his wife not answering the phone in the morning?"

"Good questions, Jackie. He told me he got stuck in Milwaukee late and he had a few drinks, so he decided to stay overnight. I confirmed that with the people he was with and the hotel records. And of course, the texts between them that night."

"But Dawn said she was with him. Did they not get

their stories straight? She could be admitting to the affair and then pulling him in to give her cover."

"Or she could have been waiting in his hotel room for him. Simple as that," Jeff said.

"True. But if they were both that far away it makes it harder. Maybe neither of them did it."

"The window Dawn gave me as to the time of death was pretty broad. If it was poisoning, the reaction time varies. So, they are both still my prime suspects. I'm meeting Judy in about fifteen minutes. Want to join us?

"Not this time, Jeff. I have a couple of things I want to check out myself. But I hope she has information that helps. Let me know what you find out."

"Jackie, don't go getting yourself in trouble. I don't want to find myself hiding behind bushes again."

"Hey, it worked, didn't it? But I take it you mean well. I'm just info gathering on this one," I said, blowing him a kiss as I walked away.

CHAPTER NINETEEN

My first stop on my way back to the studio was Dolly's Diner. Her prescient words about Kara's death stuck with me. I needed to know more.

The diner was quiet. Dolly worked on paperwork in the back booth. Perfect. It was time I asked her more about her dreams. More about what she thought happened to Kara.

"Dolly, do you have a minute?"

"Sure. Have a seat. Coffee?"

"I'd love some if it's not too much bother," I said.

She soon returned with two cups of coffee. "I've been thinking about you, Jackie. Since you've been back here in Harmony you've been involved in solving several murders. The fact we even have had several murders is unusual enough, but your part in finding the perpetrators has been amazing to me."

"You know that's not completely true. It's not like I did it myself."

Dolly held up her hand to silence my protestations. "Not necessary to explain. I think we both know what I'm talking about. Sure, you laugh and say it's just your curiosity or some such thing. Whatever it is that gets you involved, and keeps you involved, I count as a blessing. Not that our police aren't great, but it takes someone like you to sift through things, sort out the possibilities, and find the guilty party."

I chuckled at her expression. "Dolly, please. I just happen…"

She looked at me without smiling. "Jackie, you know I'm serious here. This isn't idle flattery like I sling around the diner occasionally."

"Flattery? You? Dolly, you hand out more guff to people than flattery."

Dolly raised her finger. "You might be right on that." She started laughing too. "It's hard to be taken seriously sometimes but trust me I'm serious now. Very serious."

"I'm sorry to tease you, Dolly. It's just that I'm not used to hearing these types of things from you. You and your diner are one of the most important cogs in the engine that keeps Harmony going. I'm flattered that you feel I contribute to finding the guilty ones."

I leaned closer to her, my eyes scanning the room. "Except it's not the kind of thing to spread around. We don't want Stu highlighting the number of murders here when he promotes the town in his paper."

"Point well taken," Dolly said.

"Now where were you going with those thoughts?" I asked.

"You wanted to talk to me, remember?" Dolly said.

"Oh right! I wanted to ask you more about that dream, that premonition you had. You even said you didn't think Kara's was a natural death. Why did you say that?"

"I saw you went to the funeral at the cemetery this morning," Dolly said.

"I did. But I didn't see you."

"I was there at the end. Just stayed in the background," Dolly said. "I had to pay my respects and see that Kara's remains were laid to rest. And for another reason, Jackie." Dolly sat back and crossed her arms. "The raven. I needed to see if he was there, ready to help her cross over. Didn't have any trouble seeing him. He made a big show at the funeral now, didn't he?"

"He sure did. The pastor handled it well though. But

what first made you think it wasn't natural causes like you told me?"

"I wouldn't bother telling this to anyone else. They'd laugh at my dreams and visions. That's okay. I'm good with that. The raven and Kara came to me in my dreams."

Dolly stopped and waited. I must have done something with my face that made her think I was skeptical about such a thing.

"Go on." I gave her the verbal nudge because I wanted to hear what she had to say.

"I needed to hear you say that. Let that curiosity of yours kick into high gear, Jackie, because I'm about to tell you some things and I don't know what they mean. Heck, who am I kidding. I'm not smart enough to figure it out myself. But I hope you can find a place for them in the puzzle of Kara's death."

"Go ahead. Jeff and I have gotten some more information since I last talked to you. I was hoping you could tell more about what you suspected or had a gut feeling about."

Dolly nodded and took a deep breath as though steeling herself. "I knew Kara well. She used to work here in the summers during high school and then when she came back from college. She didn't complete her degree and was at loose ends until she met Nick. He was a social climber. She was gorgeous and would look good on his arms as he climbed the ladder within the company he worked for. She was a farm girl at heart. And a beauty. Innocent. It was easy enough for him to sweep her off her feet. Sadly, a handsome worldly man crossed her path. After they'd been dating a short time, he asked her to marry him. She confided in me that her parents weren't happy about the news, so they eloped to Dubuque."

"Iowa? Who elopes to Dubuque, Iowa?" I asked.

"A little secret of the Midwest. You always hear about Las Vegas, but not Dubuque. Just cross the Mississippi and you're good to go. Her parents were fit to be tied when she showed up a married woman. Not only were they unhappy about her choice, but when they didn't get to see their daughter get married in a Lutheran ceremony at St. Paul's, it about broke their relationship with her. Rough times. I've had many conversations with her about that."

"And I can see the double blow for them now, when he wouldn't let them have a traditional Lutheran funeral, either."

"Right. I get the cremation thing if that's what she requested, but they still would have liked a church service," Dolly said. "What really got me was that he didn't want an autopsy done. And that Doc Dawn agreed with it and signed the death certificate as her dying of her heart problems. She had heart problems, over him! Kara knew he was cheating on her."

Thoughts began swirling in my head. Dolly knew about his infidelity. She loved Kara. I couldn't believe what I was thinking. The words fell from my lips. "Did you write that note?"

Dolly stared at me with an intensity that frightened me. "You mean paste it together?"

"So, you did it? For your friend?"

Dolly burst out in her familiar loud laugh. "Gotcha, Jackie. That's what I mean about you. You are always thinking."

"Dolly, this isn't funny. Why didn't you just go to Jeff with what you knew?"

Dolly shook her head with a chuckle. "I didn't write that note. But I wish I had. Smart person whoever it was. That note put the idea in folks' minds, especially the police, that it wasn't what it appeared to be. I heard about it from Dawn's receptionist. She said she talked to Kim about the magazine thing and pages missing, then Jeff coming in with questions about a note."

I sucked in a big breath. "Whew, you had me going, Dolly. I should have known the news would get out sooner than I thought. Since you weren't at the luncheon, there's something you might not have heard about."

"They liked my potato salad?" Dolly said with a wink.

"Yes. It got rave reviews as always."

"That there was another note?"

"Seriously? That was just an hour ago!"

"News like that travels fast. Did you see what it said?"

"Two words. Not natural."

"I take it you and Jeff have no idea who sent either note."

"It crossed my mind the Ericksons might have done the first note."

"Until you thought it was me?" Dolly said.

"Yes," I answered. "And it still could be. They might have made up the one they got. Thus, the big announcement at the funeral."

"I'd give that idea up. They wouldn't have made the connection to the affair. I don't think Kara would have taken that to her parents because she didn't want them pulled into the middle of the mess. Do you know I saw her the day before she was found?"

"No. Did anything seem off about her during that visit?"

"She wasn't feeling well. I attributed it to stress. She's telling me that Nick's business was having some issues and she might have to go back to work. He couldn't stand it thinking I'd just be a waitress again, she said. I saw the sparkle leaving her lovely eyes."

"Whoa…his business was in trouble. Was that common knowledge?" I asked.

"Not that I know. And Jackie, there's something else that might not be common knowledge. Do you have a moment for me to tell you?"

CHAPTER TWENTY

The evening closed in around me as I spent time on my computer at the studio. I searched online for more information regarding what Dolly told me about. Could this be what everything pointed to? Could her dreams and premonitions be right?

The more I searched the more it seemed plausible. And the more confused my mind was getting. It was hard to face, but I had to acknowledge that my brain was slowing down. I wasn't thinking clear headed. It had been a long day.

When Rocco called and asked if he could buy me a drink at Shorty's so we could talk about news in the search for my sister, I agreed. But first I had to capture the clues, the thoughts, and the possibilities flitting around in my head. I wrote things down on post-it-notes. What I knew. When I knew it. When it happened. What it could have meant. What it might mean.

It helped to write them down in a concrete form on these little squares of paper. I needed to consider each in turn and in relationship to the others. To weave the pieces into something recognizable, because it all seemed so bizarre and disjointed.

Soon an order emerged. Not enough to present to Jeff, especially at this time of night. I needed to fill in some gaps before that. But I needed to know if he heard anything new from Judy.

I reached him at home. "Judy showed up this time," he said. "She's suspected the affair for some time. But she didn't think that it was her place to say something about it. She had only been working with the doctor for a few months and didn't want to risk her job. She was getting comfortable here and loved our little town. She was making friends, including the Ericksons, because of their shared interest in natural healing."

"That would put her in a tough position, for sure," I said.

"And that's why she didn't want to speak in the office in case someone else was listening. She said that she realized she had to tell me. She couldn't keep it in anymore. When she learned about the notes circulating, she figured the word on the affair was out. Then she was beating herself up that she hadn't told someone sooner. Maybe she could have saved Kara's life. She was really shook up. I tried to tell her we don't even know it's murder yet."

"That was a good way to calm her down," I said. "So, it was more confirmation of the affair than anything else right?"

"Far as I could tell. I didn't learn anything new. She was glad we were going to send the other blood sample from Kara's body to the lab. That's about it. And soon as I get the results back from the lab on that sample and confirm that there is no so-called research project, I'll have to bring up charges against Nick and Dawn."

"You still think it's the two of them?"

"You don't?"

"I'm not sure. Apparently, you doubt the existence of a research study. Then why would Dawn take another blood sample if she wasn't authorized to, and it might point to a poison in her patient's blood?"

"I'm ahead of you on that. I'll bet she did it because, even with her denial of thinking it involved Nick in his wife's death, she wanted some insurance in case Nick backed out on her. Hung her out to dry. Or ended their affair. I'll bet the blood will show a poison. Remember, Nick was trying to get Kara to lose weight and was making protein drinks for her to take to work with her."

"I didn't know about the drinks, Jeff. When did that come up?"

"He mentioned it in one of our conversations. I didn't think much about it at the time. He sounded like a concerned husband. But when all this about poisoning came up, I figured it would be an innocent looking way to get poison into her. And thus, the quick cremation. But Nick didn't know Dawn took that last blood draw."

"I'll bet Dawn knew about the shakes and had her suspicions too," I said.

"Yep. With certain ingredients, distasteful flavors could be masked. Especially in a thick fruity drink. Enough for now. My brain hurts," Jeff said. "Are we still on for tomorrow night at Scott's? I'm looking forward to a good steak after this week."

"We certainly are. See you tomorrow."

Definitely a clue I didn't have before. Protein shakes Nick made for his wife. Maybe her own husband used those to cover the unpleasant taste of a poison? I wrote what I'd learned from Jeff on a couple more post-it-notes and added them to the colorful timeline mess in front of me.

Time to stop and meet Rocco.

I stood up and rolled my shoulders, which Libby took as a bedtime move. "Nope Libby, my sweet one. Not bedtime for me. It's time for me to head over to Shorty's and have a cold one. I won't be long."

CHAPTER TWENTY-ONE

*R*occo was already seated in a booth. He was looking over some papers spread out on the table in front of him. I stopped and ordered a Leinenkugel draft in a frosted glass.

"You meeting Rocco? Go on and sit down. I'll bring it over. Need to get some kind of exercise tonight," Shorty said, chuckling as he reached in the freezer for a frosted mug.

"Big break in the case?" I asked Rocco as I slid into the booth.

"It might be. Surprisingly, I found someone who thinks they recognize the Caroline Smith we've been looking for."

"That's great! Progress at last."

"I scoured any information from that time period about small productions in New York theater."

"It boggles my mind the things that can be found online. Where did that search lead you?"

"I discovered some historical images put online a few years ago by a small museum in the theater district of New York. It's quite a fascinating little place and they've done extensive research and archiving of productions over the decades. I reached out to them to get names of theaters in the state during the time period Caroline would have been there. One kind soul put her all into helping me and she sent me this. She believes this is a photograph of your half-sister in a theater production in New York."

Rocco slid his phone toward me so I could see the photograph. It was of a group of costumed actors. There were three men and five women.

"Which one is she?" I asked. My heart raced with the possibilities this provided us in our search.

Rocco didn't answer and instead pulled out a black-and-white photograph. "First take a close look at this. It's your mother at the approximate age of the actress. I got it from Ruth. She was probably about nineteen in this photograph."

Shorty had come up behind me with my beer. As I was trying to find some family resemblance between the two images, he noticed the photo of Joanna, my mother. "Well look at her. Joanna was just the prettiest thing. I had a crush on her when we were kids. Most everyone did," Shorty said. "What's with the trip down memory lane?"

"Shorty, do you see anyone in this cell phone photo who might be related to Joanna?" I moved over to let Shorty sit down next to me.

He took the phone and zoomed in on the picture there. Then he held it over the photograph of my mother, his eyes shifting between the two. "If I had to pick one person, I'd say the gal in the prairie bonnet. She has that beautiful hair like your mother's, and her smile. And if I'm not mistaken, you have that same smile, Jackie."

I looked at the photograph of my mother. She was sitting on the grass. A picnic? The wind blew her hair, lifting tendrils caught in the sunlight. I didn't remember my mom's hair being that wavy. She usually wore it up in a chignon. She was beautiful. Young, happy, glowing.

I reached for Rocco's phone to look at the theater group again. Now I could see what Shorty saw. That was my mother's smile.

"Who is this gal?" Shorty asked. "Some long-lost relative?"

Should I tell him the truth? Only a few people knew I even had a half-sister.

"There's a possibility," Rocco said. "Looks like that young man wants to pay his bill."

"Hey Sid, I'm coming," Shorty said.

As soon as Shorty stepped away, Rocco said, "I distracted him because I wasn't sure you wanted to say more yet."

I told Rocco, "Thanks. I didn't see it at first, but he knew my mom as a young girl. So, is that the woman who might be Caroline?"

"Yes, according to the woman at the museum," Rocco said.

Sid? It hit me. I spun to look at the man Shorty was with. It was him. The groundskeeper from Taliesin. The man Kara feared was stalking her. He was paying his bill. He'd be leaving the bar. I couldn't just stop him and ask him questions like why he didn't go back to work after her body was found. Think quick, Jackie. Engage him somehow.

"I'll be right back," I said to Rocco before grabbing my beer and walking up next to Sid at the bar. "Hey Shorty, you gave me the wrong beer," I said before turning to smile at Sid. "I'm not a beer connoisseur but I knew that wasn't what I wanted."

Ignoring Shorty's surprised expression I said, "I

recognize you. You work at Taliesin. Those grounds are huge. You must be busy with fall cleanup."

I realized my mistake when with a nod he turned and hurried out the back door. Ask questions if you want to engage someone in a conversation...but don't scare them off.

"That's the beer you ordered," Shorty said.

"I know. Sorry. I was trying to get Sid to talk to me. Do you know him?"

"Not really, but I know the guy he rents from. He brought Sid with him one night. Then the kid came in a couple of times by himself. Stopped in tonight. Said he's moving out tomorrow. People don't get him. He's an unusual looking guy and not the brightest bulb. He's really more like a kid. He has no filters. Socially awkward is what Lon called it."

"Why did he leave out the back way?"

"His apartment is up on Oak Street, so it's a shortcut. What did you want to talk to him about?"

"I just wanted to meet him. He knew the woman who died at Taliesin."

"Sad to hear when someone so young goes. And here I am hanging around past my prime," Shorty joked.

. . .

occo offered to walk me home after we finished our drinks. We left by the back door as well because it went out to the alleyway and led to the back entrance to my apartment above the studio. The air was much colder now, and the wind howled between the buildings.

"I can't thank you enough for discovering that theater photograph. Have you shown it to Aunt Ruth yet?"

"I sent her a copy in an email, but I want to have a copy printed to take to the Shady Pines team. They can compare them side by side and see the resemblance like Shorty did."

"This feels like a solid lead. I can't tell you how much I appreciate all you're doing."

"Maybe we could get together tomorrow night and show the gals," Rocco said.

"Scott's doing a cookout for some friends. I'd love to be there but…" I stopped in my tracks. There on my garage door, scratched in the finish, were the words *stay out of it* in crude stick letters.

"Jacqueline, what could this mean? It's threatening. We should call the police chief immediately."

"No. Wait. I think I know what it is about. It's so late, Jeff's probably at home watching the news. I have a hunch. Could we walk the long way back to your boat? If my hunch is right, we might encounter the person who did this."

"Does this have to do with that man we just saw at Shorty's? Do you think he did this? If you do, I'm calling Jeff."

"I don't think it was him. But I think I know who. If you'll come with me, Rocco, and if I'm right, you can call Jeff then."

CHAPTER TWENTY-TWO

The only window on the street side of the doctor's office was in the entry door. I saw a dim square of light behind the receptionist's desk. Rocco and I walked around to the rear where an older sedan was parked. I'd explained to Rocco what I was going to do if things went as planned.

"Looks like you were right about her being here," he said.

"I hope so. Also, could be someone cleaning the office. Let's see."

The rear door was unlocked, so we walked in.

She looked up, startled to see anyone coming in from the back. "Jackie. Hi. Can I help you with something?"

"No. Mr. Montalvo and I noticed the lights on, and we were concerned, as it's highly unusual," I said.

"I'm just straightening out some records before I leave. I don't want the patients to be at a loss. We're having temporary staff from Greensville come in and help out."

"So, it's true? I'm sure the doctor is sorry to see you go. Does she know the truth about why you're leaving?"

"I didn't go into great detail. I just made up some sort of excuse about my son finding a better job and that I wanted to move to be near him. It seemed pointless to say more about it."

"We just saw your son at Shorty's and heard you were moving. He seems like such a gentle soul."

Judy jerked her head in my direction. "You did?"

I'd caught her off guard. Good.

"Most people don't see that in him, but thank you for saying it."

Before she had a chance to say anything more, I spoke. "I understand he's had some issues before. That's a shame. People can be so cruel, can't they? Are you concerned since there's been some questioning about the cause of Kara's death and your son is being looked at? Staff at Taliesin mentioned he made her nervous, and they remarked that Kara felt he was stalking her. I thought he was probably just looking out for her because she'd walk alone in the evening."

"Is that so? I wasn't aware. I hope they direct their

efforts elsewhere," Judy snipped. "Now, if you'll excuse me, I'd like to file these remaining records."

"Certainly. I'm glad everything is okay here. Were you looking for the blood sample the doctor wanted you to ship to the lab tomorrow? It's interesting that the possibility of a poisoning has come up, don't you think?"

"Dr. Dawn asked me to handle that, so I did a quick search for it. I couldn't find it, so she'll just have to take care of it herself."

"But isn't the blood sample why you're here, Judy?"

Judy nervously shuffled the papers on the desk in front of her. She turned away from us. "No, it is not. Now, please, I need to work. Goodnight, Jackie and…"

"Rocco Montalvo," I said. "He's a friend of mine."

"Whatever. Good night."

"I know Kara's parents appreciated your efforts to help them. They'll miss you, I'm sure. It surprised me you weren't at the funeral."

"I couldn't make it. But I shared my condolences when I saw them last night."

"Oh. Yes. You brought them tea and their mail. Too bad about that note being in with their mail. Where will you move to?"

She took a deep breath before turning to face us with a forced smile.

"Probably over to the Fox Valley."

"A lovely area," Rocco remarked. "I wish you good luck there. Shall we go now, Jacqueline?"

"Sure. I need to get home to Libby. You take care, Judy."

"Thank you," Judy mumbled as she spun back around to her desk and started her pointless shuffling of papers again.

"Oh, Judy. About Kara's parents. I obtained some of the tea you'd been treating Kara with. It's quite bitter. What was it for?"

"It was a mix of herbs to calm her."

"Herbs? When the analysis on the tea is complete, I've got a feeling that they will find a floral component."

Judy's spine stiffened, but she didn't turn back to face me.

"How much foxglove was in the tea, Judy? Did you think it was just a little amount so it would only make her sick? Or did you intend to kill her?"

A small gasp escaped from the defeated figure at the desk. Judy's shoulders rolled down, her head bent forward. Seconds ticked by until she said, "I didn't intend to kill her."

"Shall I call Jeff now?" Rocco said.

"Yes, please," I said.

CHAPTER TWENTY-THREE

he hunch I'd gone on was right. The gamble paid off. Could we have proven Judy's guilt without her confession? Maybe. The blood sample after death might show an overdose of digitalis from the tea laced with foxglove. But it was Judy's confession that sealed it.

Jeff showed up at the doctor's office. After talking to Judy, he agreed to let her go back home to be with her son for the night. He confiscated her car keys and drove her to her apartment.

Rocco walked away toward the marina and his temporary home on the *Roccome Baby* after I thanked him profusely for being there to witness Judy's confession.

I went home to Libby, who was now snoring softly at

my feet. A hot chocolate and Aunt Ruth's crocheted afghan warmed me as I sat on my balcony. I'm excited the week is winding down and things can get back to normal. Tomorrow night at Scott's for a cookout with a few friends was something to look forward to.

It was getting too cold and blustery to sit outside anymore tonight though. I was relaxed enough to get a good sleep. When I went in, I saw I'd missed a call from Scott. This didn't bode well. It wasn't like him to call at this late hour.

I picked up the voice message...*Jackie, baby Drake is on his way! We're at the hospital now. Mandy's contractions are getting stronger and more frequent. Baby will be here soon. I want you here with me to celebrate this birth. Please come Xoxoxo Scott I'll leave your name at the front desk.*

He wanted me to be there? I felt my heart swell in my chest. He wanted me at the birth of his grandchild. I tried calling him back but didn't get an answer. They might not be able to take phone calls in the room. I quickly texted him...*I just picked this up on my way.* Then in a random act I added...*love J*

I brushed my teeth. After pulling my hair up into a bun, I freshened my makeup. Not bad for an old lady after midnight, I thought. He wants you there!

Should I change clothes? I was still in the black dress I'd worn to the funeral. Most definitely yes. I stripped the dress over my head and slipped into a cream turtle-neck and jeans, grabbing my rust-colored barn jacket.

As I backed out my headlights shone on the garage door and the message scratched in it. A reminder of all that happened in the past couple of hours. The woman who'd done the damage would do no more.

And I was on my way to be with people I loved to welcome a baby into our world. With a smile plastered on my face I kept replaying the fact that Scott wanted me with him at the birth of his first grandchild. That's a pretty big thing.

The sign on the locked front doors told me the only available entrance at this time of night was through the Emergency Department. Now where was that? I'd never been here before.

The parking lot signs directed me to circle the building where I found arrows pointing me to the Emergency Department parking lot. There were several other cars there, including Scott's pickup truck with the words Drake Construction on the door.

Mandy's having her baby and he wants me here!

I checked my lip gloss in the rearview mirror before walking through the windy and dimly lit lot toward the canopy announcing the Emergency Department Entrance. For the first time I felt hesitation. Were things going okay for Mandy?

The woman behind the desk peered at me over her reading glasses. "May I help you?"

"I'm Jackie Parker."

"Okay. Are you by yourself? Do you need a wheelchair, or can you walk back to the emergency room?"

"Oh no. I'm here for Mandy Drake. She's in the maternity wing I guess."

"She's having her baby?"

"Yes. I'm on some sort of list, I was told."

The woman reached across her desk for a paper. "Hmm…I don't see you here. I have a Jacqueline Drake, but no Jackie Parker."

Realizing that Scott had made me a close relative in order to get in, I said, "Oh I'm sorry. Yes, that's me. I use my last name professionally and it slips out sometimes."

"Well then, congratulations, Mrs. Drake, on the impending birth of your grandchild." She gave me a badge with the name Jacqueline Drake and the word Grandmother already printed on it."

My fingers nervously took it from her and clipped it to the lapel on my jacket. He wants me here with him and his family.

The hospital was eerily quiet. Hushed. The ER receptionist gave me a map, but I still got turned around. When I ended up at the desk of the pediatric ward, I finally stopped to ask a nurse where the newborns were.

She got me back on track and I found myself at the maternity ward doors, which were closed and locked.

Through the window I could see a short way down the hall. A nurse's station formed the center hub of the maternity wing. I pressed a button and announced who I was. I realized someone was watching me on a camera because they asked me to hold my badge up against the scanner. With a soft hum, the door to the ward opened.

Stepping in, the same quiet calm prevailed. Until the piercing cry of a baby came from a room to my right. Was that Baby Drake? My path toward the nurse's station took me past the newborn nursery. Four swaddled infants rested in their bassinets. A fifth baby was being held and rocked by a grandmotherly figure.

A young woman in a hospital gown stood looking through the window and into the nursery. She gazed adoringly at an infant in a small pink cap asleep in one of the bassinets.

"What did you name her?" I asked.

"Isabella, after her grandmother. We're going to call her Izzy. I couldn't sleep. All I want to do is stare at her."

"She's beautiful. So precious. Your first?"

The woman nodded. "Thank you. She is perfect. All ten toes and ten fingers. Are you here for a birth?"

"Yes, my manager is…"

I stopped as the woman glanced at my name badge.

"Oh, I see. Congratulations Grandma! Prayers that all goes well. Boy or girl?"

"A boy. But I'm not really…"

"You hurry along now. I'm sure they are looking for you."

"Yes. They are," I said. I turned, and there, down a long sterile hospital corridor, stood Scott with a big smile and open welcoming arms.

I walked toward him thinking, he wants me here, and I want to be here.

CHAPTER TWENTY-FOUR

Patti and Charlie were in the waiting area, as were Mandy's parents.

"She's resting now, but if things proceed as they have been, another contraction will come soon. It's been waves and then quiet," Patti said.

"They are monitoring the baby and he's not under stress, so things will just take time," Matt said. "We're so glad to see you here, Jackie."

"Thank you. Mandy means the world to me and I'm glad to be here. Even as a fake Grandma." I laughed. "How did you account for three grandmothers getting in?"

Scott laughed. "I was worried about that. I wanted you here earlier but thought it wouldn't fly with Nurse Ratchet on the floor at the time. When shifts changed we got a new nurse. She was the one who let us know that there are so many stepfamily situations now that they just ask for people to identify as grandmother, grandfather, brother or sister. No biggie. No explanation needed."

"Though she cautioned us not to go overboard and have six grandmas here before the night is over," Mandy's mother said. "I can imagine she saw a handsome eligible bachelor like you, Scott and figured you might have a few special friends."

Scott blushed. "I'm a one woman at a time guy." He put his arm around me as we sat next to each other on the sofa. "I assured her you were the only other grandmother who would show up."

Patti just shook her head. "I know Mandy will be happy you're here."

"How long has she been here?" I asked.

"Matt brought her in about three hours ago when her water broke," Mandy's mother said.

"So, all the while we've been sitting here, what have you been up to?" Patti asked. "I saw you at the funeral and the luncheon. I'm sorry I didn't get to talk to you more. Wasn't that strange about Martin making that announcement?"

"What announcement?" Scott asked.

"That he and Inis had received an anonymous note about their daughter's death."

Mandy's parents looked puzzled, so Patti explained what had been happening.

"Mandy said nothing to us about this. But then I guess we are always so busy with baby stuff. I had no idea. Who did the other one go to?" Mandy's father asked.

"To Kim Walters, the realtor," I said. "And then there was another on my garage door tonight telling me to stay out of it."

Scott pulled back to look at me. "You had a threatening note, and you didn't call me right away? Never let that happen again. You know I worry about you getting involved in dangerous situations."

"I appreciate your concern, Scott, but I'm a grown woman. I can handle myself. Plus, I've been living in big cities and have gained street smarts too."

"Hey now, first argument. Aren't they cute?" Patti teased. "Don't let his gallant knight in shining armor throw you off, Jackie. He's that way with anyone he cares about."

"Sorry if it came across wrong, Jackie. Having lived in a big city gives you an edge to deal with different situations, but you've got to admit there have been an extraordinary amount of death investigations lately. And you've found yourself in the middle of most of them. How many murder investigations did you deal with in Chicago?" Scott said.

"Well besides the crime scene photos I took early in my career, zero," I said. "You have a point. Okay worry-wart, if I ever get another threatening note, you'll be the first to know." I kissed his cheek to seal the deal.

"You look like you've had a long day, Jackie," Scott whispered. "How about you lean against my shoulder and catch a little sleep?"

"I'm wound up. Don't think I can sleep," I said, leaning up against him.

"Just try. Believe me, I'll let you know if anything develops," Scott said as he stroked my head.

The waiting area lights dimmed. I noticed Mandy's father's soft snores from across the room after Mandy's mom went into the birthing room to be with her daughter. Charlie had to go home and get some rest for a case in the morning. Patti went downstairs to walk out with him and get coffee from the vending area.

The next thing I knew I felt Scott's gentle squeeze. "Wake up. They called Matt into the birthing room because the baby is on his way!"

I sat up and rubbed my eyes just as Matt came around the corner. "He's almost here! I can't believe it's finally happening."

Scott and Patti both hugged their son. "Now off with you. Your wife needs you."

Within minutes a nurse came to tell us Mandy and Matt had a healthy baby boy. And that mother and baby were doing fine.

"How's father doing?" Scott asked.

"He's okay too," she laughed. "He'll come out and get you soon."

It wasn't long until Matt appeared in the waiting area. "Sorry you had to wait. They needed to clean baby and Mandy up. He's the cutest little guy! You all can come in now."

Mandy looked radiant holding her son. What a miracle. To see a brand new little person. Scott and Patti wrapped their arms around their son. Mandy's parents were beaming on the other side of the bed. Charlie, dressed in his suit for work, made his way into the room and Patti ran to him saying what a perfect little baby he was.

Scott came toward me with moist eyes. "I am in awe of what a gift we have been given. To be grandparents to this little man. To see my son become a father. And to have his son in our life."

I smiled up at him. "It is a blessing. I am indescribably happy for you."

"For us," Scott said.

"Just look at Mandy's parents, and this isn't even their first grandchild. Can I go sneak a closer peak now?"

"Come on Jackie. I don't think Mandy even realizes you're here in the room."

"I didn't want to push my way past the grandparents."

"You're not pushing anything. But maybe I should be. You were the person I wanted to be here with me tonight. And I want you by my side to help take care of this little guy the first time I babysit. And I want us to have a party for him on his first birthday. I want him to know you and love you. Just like I do."

CHAPTER TWENTY-FIVE

That walking on air feeling was still with me as I left the hospital to go home and get some sleep. It was a new day.

I'd reached Todd earlier to open up the studio and take Libby out in the back fenced area for me. I still couldn't believe my luck in getting Todd to work with us during Mandy's maternity leave, and fingers crossed he would stay for much longer.

"Todd, you're a doll. It's been a long night. Baby and mom are both resting."

"No problem, Jackie. I'm just thrilled everything went well with the birth," he said.

"Me too. Especially with the early delivery. I'm heading up to sleep for a few hours. Napping on the couch of a hospital waiting room just doesn't cut it for someone my age."

"Oh no you don't slip away, not until I hear the name they decided on."

"Tyrone Scott Drake. Ty for short. Isn't it cute?"

"Whoa that's quite a handle for a little guy."

"It's Mandy's father's middle name and of course the Scott connection you know."

"Speaking of the Scott connection. How's that going? Did you two spend the night together?" Todd asked in a coy suggestive tone.

"Todd! That's a very intimate question to be asking me," I said. "But yes, we did. He was right next to me on that couch waiting for baby Ty to arrive. Now off to a real bed, for me. I'll be back down in five hours. And do not wake me for anything."

"Unless there's blood?"

I laughed. "Yes, unless there's blood."

After my nap and a long shower, I was ready to start the day that most people of Harmony were halfway through. Including Jeff. He texted me that Judy Hobbs requested me to be at the station at one o'clock.

I called him. "Are you sure she wants to see me? I'm surprised. I thought she would be furious with me."

"She wants you to know that she holds no grudge. She owes you an apology for the damage she did to your garage door. But I've got a sense she's almost grateful you caught her. Her remorse at doing what she did was real. I hope you'll come."

"I'll be there by one."

"Here's my Sleeping Beauty," Todd said as I came down from my upstairs apartment. "That warm jacket you're wearing must mean you're heading out."

"I am. I'll have you know that besides being with Mandy last night, I also helped solve a murder case."

"Say what? The body they found on Tuesday when you and Mandy were at Taliesin?"

"Yes. Kara Davis was poisoned. And with a little help from my friends, I figured out who did it."

"I'll bet it was the person who scratched that warning in your garage door. Am I right?"

"Yep. But how did you see that?"

"Remember I put Libby out in your postage stamp-sized back yard to do her morning business. So, spill. What happened? Going from natural causes to murder by poison in what, three or four days?"

"I'll catch you up with the news later. Everything okay here?"

"It is. Now don't be mad. You told me not to wake you and I respected that command. But you missed a visitor."

"Who was this visitor?"

"Alli Turner! Can you believe it? I recognized her right away. We've been friends on social media for years, but I've never met her in person."

"Aren't you glad you decided to work here? We're a happening place."

"Yes I am. Her mother was with her. Stunning woman. She's an actress as well. But I don't watch soap operas so I'm not familiar with her. This film is going to be based on the memoir she wrote. *Becoming Beverly*. It sounds interesting. Beverly was her mother's name, and she took it as her stage name."

"I'm sorry I missed them."

"I'm hoping they'll agree to let me blog about their movie to promote Harmony," Todd said.

"Did they like the studio?"

"Oh yes. They even bought some prints that they want Mandy to frame for them when she's back. They are leaving tomorrow, but I put myself out there and invited them to dinner, or should I say supper? At the Stone Mill tonight. And guess what?"

"They said yes?"

"No, they said no, smarty pants. But only because…

they'll already be there to meet with…drum roll please…"

I managed a fake drumroll sound before he said, "Your Aunt Ruth! And of course, the Shady Pines gals too."

"What? Oh my gosh, Ruth will be so happy. Beverly used to play Pauline Dubois in Times of Our Life. Ruth's favorite soap opera."

"So I heard. Kay arranged it for them. I plan on party crashing at their table. Oh, and Val came from next door with a copy of her memoir and had Beverly sign it."

"Did Val happen to mention her hair salon being stuck in the seventies?" I asked. "And might they like to use it in the movie?"

"She did, and they left with her to check it out," Todd said. "You missed all sorts of action here."

"Sounds like it. But my nap more than made up for it. Bye for now, Todd."

I gave Scott a call on the way to the police station but got his answering machine. When his voice mail message came up, I suggested we meet Kay and Jeff at Stone Mill instead of cooking out, as it had been such a late night. Secretly, I wanted to meet this television star before she left town.

CHAPTER TWENTY-SIX

eff and Judy were in the station conference room with an interior window to the front desk area. I saw Jeff rise as I came in. No two-way mirrors. No hard top metal table. No bright bare overhead lightbulb. Just a thirty-year-old conference table, padded straight-back chairs, and a fluorescent light fixture.

"Sit down, Jackie. Can I get you some coffee? Or I have bottled water in the back."

"Coffee would be perfect." And I was grateful he had it. Might not be the freshest, but I could use the pick me up.

Judy looked rough. I certainly couldn't blame her with what she was facing. I suppose she'd get a lawyer to plead down the charge claiming it was unintentional.

That she didn't mean to kill Kara, just slow her down. That could very well be true. I sipped my coffee, not wanting to say the first words because I wasn't sure why I was here. Judy didn't need to explain anything to me. Inis and Martin Erickson should be here. Nick Davis should be here.

Jeff stacked a few papers he had spread in front of him, neatly put them into a folder, and moved it aside. "Judy, would you like me to leave the room and let you talk to Jackie privately?"

"No sir, no need to leave. I just wanted to thank Jackie for cornering me like she did. My last act of creeping in the alley and scratching those words in your garage door was one of desperation. I saw my son coming out of the tavern and walking home. And then it hit me. What my actions were putting him through by moving again. Running away. It wasn't his fault. Only I knew he might be in the police radar. He had no idea. He is such an innocent."

She let out an enormous sigh before continuing. "I only meant well for him. He was always different from the other boys. My husband never understood. Sid grew up big and strong. You saw him. Such a good-looking kid. At least in my eyes. But in his father's eyes, Sid was next to worthless. He was soft. He needed to fight the kids who bullied him. Sid didn't understand those things. He tried to make friends at school. Tried to be nice. As a mother it was so hard to watch. The school counselors explained his IQ was low and that he was socially immature. I remember watching my husband during that meeting. I could see he was ready to burst. He held his temper in that room, but as soon as we got home it exploded and he directed it all at Sid." Judy covered her face. A sob escaped her. She accepted the tissue Jeff offered her and collected herself.

"This explanation isn't for sympathy for me. I know that what I did to that woman is unforgivable."

"Please continue, Judy. You don't have to, but you might want to get it off your chest," Jeff said.

"It might help us help your son too," I said. "If I understand correctly, he'll need some emotional support through the things you'll both be facing."

Judy nodded. "He will. Eventually the situation at home got so bad. I fled with my son, and we've been on the move since. My driving desire was for us to find a place where he was safe. Where he was understood and appreciated. Where he could be my wonderful gentle giant and people would accept him as he was. This was probably the closest to that place that we found. Mark and the staff at Taliesin were great in the beginning. Sid loved working outdoors. He didn't have to interact with many people. His supervisor understood him." Judy looked up at me. "My landlord did too. I know you've met him, haven't you? That's where you saw the late flowering foxglove wasn't it?"

"Yes Judy, it was. But go on. What happened that made you ready to flee again?" I asked.

"Sid didn't crave being around people, but he wanted some human interaction besides his mom. Especially as he grew older. I became more overbearing, always fearful his father would find us and want to be back in his life. I also was afraid that Sid would be misunderstood or misread someone's attention. Then the bad things would happen."

"Did that happen here?" Jeff asked.

Judy stood and began pacing, wringing her hands as she walked back and forth in the small space. "Sid was a grown man in some ways and a child in others. I could tell he looked differently at Kara. She was nothing but kind to him at first. I'm sure he misunderstood what her talking with him meant. How she saw it differently than he did."

"How did you learn about him interacting with Kara?" I asked. "Did she know you were his mother?"

"I don't think so. I met Kara and her parents through my job. The first I heard about Sid knowing Kara was from Inis. We got to talking about natural, homeopathic healing which I've always practiced. It angered my husband that I wouldn't give Sid drugs but made teas and natural herbal drinks for him. But back to now. When I visited them at the farm, they'd say Kara was getting stressed out. We'd chat, like friends, you know."

"In talking with you about Kara's stress, they told you about her becoming concerned about someone at Taliesin who made her nervous?"

Judy nodded.

"I knew right away it was my son. They didn't even know his name. But with a couple of questions, I knew it was Sid."

"But why not just find a different job for Sid? He'd have forgotten about her."

"He was changing. When I saw him in the alley last night, I stepped out so he would see me. He looked from me to the garage. What I'd felt creeping into our relationship recently, I clearly saw in his eyes at that moment. Disgust. I'd seen hurt, painful emotions, but never that look. He knew I'd done it. It almost completely broke me to see him walk off without saying a word."

"When I found you at the office, what were you thinking?" I said.

"I guess I went into self-protection mode. I was losing my son. After all I'd done to protect him. The times I'd pulled him out of the big cruel world were probably over. I was smothering him."

"So, you were going to destroy the evidence? That last blood test."

"Yes. I never meant to kill Kara and Sid would never have hurt her. His feelings might have been hurt, but he would never have hurt her. The others never understood that either. The girl in Geneva. The one in Rockford. They all pointed fingers at him. Accusing him of doing things that weren't true. Can you even understand how that tore me apart? I would not go through that again. I wanted her to get a little sick. Winter was coming. She wouldn't be walking at Taliesin anymore. If I could just make it until then, Sid would forget about her. Things would be okay. When they found her body, I knew it might have been an overdose from the tea."

Listening to Judy's story I imagined she was rehearsing for a jury or a judge. I still didn't understand why I needed to hear all of this.

"I had to protect Sid. They'd think he did something to her. Suffocated her maybe. I needed to find a way out of this. If I exposed the affair, they would blame the doctor. She was wrong to be involved with Nick. He wasn't a nice man. Martin was right. I had to contaminate that second blood sample before it went out so the test wouldn't show the excess digitalis."

Jeff turned to me. "Jackie, how did you discover this possibility about the digitalis?"

"Inis used the phrase too much of a good thing when talking about Kara drinking the bitter tea Judy made for her."

Judy cringed.

"You told her to put sugar in it, didn't you, Judy? You knew she'd drink it then. Her mother trusted you. They welcomed you into their home. How could you?"

Jeff tried to steer me away from my building anger by asking, "What was the last puzzle piece for you, Jackie?"

"The morning they found the body, Mandy's photograph caught a figure near the body. Later, when we looked at the photographs of the tower, I found out who the person was and that he worked at Taliesin. I did not know he was your son. Why was he there that morning? He was supposed to be working by the main house."

Judy bit her lip and let out a long sigh. "Ah, so that's how he came into the picture for you. I'd been wondering about that."

"Why was he on that hill that morning, Judy? And why did he leave the grounds?" Jeff asked.

"On Monday, the restoration team had worked on the tower. One of them left a toolbox behind. Tuesday morning they were working in the main house. When they saw Sid on his way into work, one of them asked him to take an ATV up to the tower and grab the tools left behind. That's why my son was seen there. He noticed the commotion and as he was leaving heard about Kara's body being found. He freaked out and called me crying."

"I remember someone on an ATV, but I didn't notice what he looked like. So that was Sid, and he knew what happened?"

Judy nodded. "He was so upset to hear about his friend. I went and picked him up. My first thought right then was to protect my son."

"I assume you created the notes to point away from your son. Am I right?" Jeff asked.

Judy said, "Yes. I did. I wanted the affair to be found out. To point to Nick and Dawn."

"Did you ever seriously think they did it?" I asked.

"No," Judy murmured. "It was a misdirection. Look over there, not here. But I knew my son didn't do it either."

"I was with Rocco at Shorty's last night when I saw Sid. The man who'd been stalking Kara. Shorty said he was a nice kid, just misunderstood. He even used your phrase. Socially awkward. He left by the back door into the alley and Shorty told me he lived in an apartment on Oak Street. The landlord told Kim and I yesterday that the tenants were moving out. So, there it was. The final missing puzzle piece."

"That's quite a fluke. Still, I'll have to chew on all this to get it all," Jeff said. "You amaze me, Jackie."

"Thanks, I guess. But it was luck too. Sid had to decide to have one last beer at Shorty's before they left town. I had to be there with Rocco. Otherwise, Judy and Sid could have been gone."

"I still had the blood test though, remember. We would have found out the meds were out of whack. At least Judy here didn't get her hands on that."

"True," I said. "But no other poison would have been shown. And raised levels of digoxin could have been explained away."

Judy's eyes moved sadly between Jeff and me. "It doesn't matter now. I'm so sorry I did this to people who trusted me. I've taken something from the Ericksons that they can never get back. What I did as a mother protecting her son, has left another mother heartbroken."

CHAPTER TWENTY-SEVEN

left the police station with a bitter taste in my mouth. I know Judy didn't mean for Kara to die, just make her sick. How sick? Sick enough to be bed ridden? Sick enough not to take walks at Taliesin? Sounds like a lame story to me.

Scott had called. His voicemail said the Stone Mill would be perfect for tonight and that he would let Kay and Jeff know. Mandy and Ty were doing fine and were resting. He was going to stop up at the hospital after our dinner and hoped I'd go with him.

That brightened my mood. Walking past the Harmony Happenings office I noticed Stuart inside. He might have heard about the arrest and would ask me for comments, but I honestly didn't want to think about it anymore today. However, as I turned the corner to head to the studio, I almost ran into Kim.

"Jackie! Just the person I wanted to see. We got her, didn't we?"

I wondered how she had found out so soon. But then I remembered I'd napped the day away while word was flying through Harmony.

"I will swallow some of my pride and say that I thought it was Dr. Dawn," Kim said.

"That's who Jeff suspected too. Being part of a team means each person brings something to the table. Because you are a socially active and alert person, they sent you the first note, and you solved where it came from," I said. "Eventually it led to Judy."

Kim stood a little straighter. "You're right. Having such high visibility in the community and relationships with so many has a priceless value. My sweet Stu said he's so proud of how I always put myself out there…law of attraction he calls it. Isn't he cute? Listen, I'm meeting Rocco later to show him the Hobbs apartment. It's really lovely. Though now there will be a taint to it knowing the murder plot was hatched there. And even perhaps a lingering essence of drying flowers and herbs. The very thing that killed that poor woman." Kim shivered. "I don't know if I'd want it. But the landlord said he'd paint all the walls and wax the wood floors to freshen the place up."

"Kim, that's terrific to hear. I love that street. I hope Rocco takes the apartment, so he'll be around more this winter."

"Me too. Stu and I are taking a small gift up to Mandy, Matt and their new peanut. Have you seen the little guy?"

"Yes, I have. He is adorable. I'm going up again later tonight."

"With Grandpa Scott? You two are too cute together. So, are we going to be calling you Grandma now? Or Nana or Nonna or whatever the kids are using?"

"Funny you should ask. I was playing the role of grandmother last night to be allowed on the maternity ward at such a late hour."

"You cheated at something? Jackie, I'm surprised," Kim said, shaking her finger at me. "Don't go slipping into a life of crime."

"Very funny. A nurse suggested that Scott do it."

"I'm just kidding you, my dear. And besides, the way I see it, things are looking like you will be a step-grandma one of these days. Bye for now," Kim said, as she headed to Stuart's office.

I couldn't resist stopping in at the diner to let Dolly

know about what happened with the information she shared.

"After we talked yesterday, I did some online researching on digitalis. You were right all along about it not being a normal heart episode," I told her.

"I'm so glad that speaking up helped. My dream about Kara wandering in a field of flowers and then falling asleep there like Dorothy in the Wizard of Oz meant something?"

"And so did the fact that you knew the flowers were foxglove and not the poppies like in the Land of Oz."

"Thank goodness for Granny. As a child she told me so many tales about those fairy flowers, as she called them. But she cautioned me I must be careful because they contained powerful medicine that had been used for centuries. But that too much of it was a bad thing. I'm so glad you listened and figured it out."

"I only researched the possibility of the flowers because of your dream, Dolly. I remembered meeting Lon on Oak Street and him pointing out the foxglove on their second bloom. I didn't know Judy rented from him at that point. But I did know that Judy gave Kara a tea to help calm her stress. When your dream included foxglove, the pieces started fitting together. Dolly, you and your dreams helped me to discover the truth."

. . .

At the studio, Todd was closing things up for the day. He was excited to meet up with Beverly and Alli Turner at the Stone Mill tonight. His cheerful upbeat personality was just what I needed now. No more talk about poisonous flowers today.

"Before the supper meetup tonight, I'm off to see my girl, Mama Mandy and her new little person. How did your afternoon go?"

No way was I going back down that road. "Great! In fact, I'll see you later, my friend. Since last night neither Scott nor I got much sleep, we're meeting our friends Kay and Jeff for dinner at the Stone Mill as well."

"Oh wonderful! You can see your aunt get all fan girl over Beverly."

Upstairs Libby waited. I showered and dressed. As I listened to Al Green while doing up my hair, I kept finding her underfoot. She suspected something was up. "Sorry girl. I know I left you too long last night. But I'll be a little late again tonight. I'm going to visit your new little buddy, Ty. Wait until you meet him. I think you two will hit it off."

CHAPTER TWENTY-EIGHT

The first people I noticed at the Stone Mill were Rocco and Lon, the landlord from Oak Street. They must have struck a deal for the apartment. The third person sitting with them was none other than Sid Hobbs.

"Jacqueline! May I introduce my soon to be landlord, Lon Harper and his current tenant, Sid Hobbs."

I extended my hand to Lon and said, "Nice to see you again." I turned toward Sid and brushed aside all I'd heard today. "And Sid, it's nice to see you out for the evening."

I lost my hand in his big rough one, but the feel was that of, what Judy called him, a gentle giant. "Nice to meet you."

Lon smiled. "Rocco loves the apartment and has just

signed a lease, so we are celebrating. I'm happy to say Sid here is going to be staying with me for a while. We'll have an upstairs neighbor, right Sid?"

"Yes sir," Sid said.

No mention of his mother. Good.

"In fact, Sid here will help me prep the greenhouse Kate and I have outside of town." Lon reached over and patted Sid on the shoulder. "He's happy working with plants and will be a great asset there."

Sid smiled shyly, ducking his head. "I like plants."

"And Rocco, I'm so happy you found a place here in Harmony. I don't think I could bear seeing your boat go into storage and you drive off to Chicago."

"Thank you for those kind words, Jacqueline. This is a load off my mind. Are you meeting anyone here tonight? I see the Shady Pines gals are part of a large group or I would have gone over and shared my good news with them," Rocco said. "I thought you were going to be at Scott's for a cookout."

"Plans changed. I'm meeting Scott, Jeff, and Kay for dinner here. And then afterward Scott and I are running back up to the hospital to see his new grandson."

"I had not heard the baby arrived," Rocco said. "Congratulations to Mandy and Matt. So has reality sunk in yet for Scott?"

From behind, two arms wrapped around me. "It sure

has. And if I have my way, this gorgeous woman will help me with the whole grandparent thing. I have a great deal to learn."

I leaned back against him, soaking in what he said.

"But now I'm going to steal her away to join our friends."

"You're a wise man, Scott Drake," Rocco said, raising his wine glass. "Cheers."

Scott kept his arm around my shoulder as we walked past Ruth's table. "Scott, can you give me a minute? I want to introduce myself to those women sitting with the Shady Pine gals."

"Want me to go with you?"

"No, it's okay. But order me the Pulp Man Ale. I'll be right over."

The chatter and laughter at the table made it obvious this group was enjoying their evening. Todd had managed to get himself seated next to Alli. Her mother Beverly was in between Ruth and Betty. She was a beautiful woman. Her rich brown hair was in a stylish cut that cost more than all the haircuts Val did at Cut-n-Curl in a week.

Dorothy noticed me first. "Jackie, I don't know if you'll be able to get a word in with the way those three are going at it. This was the best surprise. Kay told me to get them here. I think she thought I was the only one who could keep the surprise."

I finally caught my aunt's eye.

"Jackie honey! Look who Kay arranged for us to meet."

"I see. Can you introduce me?"

"Oh of course. Silly me. This is Beverly Turner, also known as the famous Pauline Dubois. I've been telling her I can't believe she showed up in our little village. This is so exciting."

"Nice to meet you, Jackie," Beverly said. "Your aunt has been telling me about you. I was in your studio and saw some of your work. You're a talented artist."

"Thank you. Todd mentioned that you and your daughter were in today. I understand you two might be making a movie in Harmony. If there's anything we can do to help facilitate the process, please don't hesitate to ask."

"Everyone has been so welcoming. We are overwhelmed," Beverly said.

I nodded to Alli. "You are making quite a stir with your visits to our little village. Everyone has been following your progress in scouting for locations."

"You all are so sweet and making it easier to convince my mother that this can happen. Ever since I read her memoir and began exploring her story, I've wanted to bring her here."

Ruth said, "How on earth did you choose this town to do the filming in?"

"May I tell them?" Alli asked her mother.

Beverly fidgeted with a large diamond ring on her finger. "I don't know, dear. It might be a little soon. After all, we are guests here tonight and it might not be the right moment."

"We will have to talk about it some time, Mom." Alli looked around the table. "These are the women who would know about that time."

"True," Beverly said, giving her daughter a tight smile. "But I wish you wouldn't put me on the spot like this, Allison."

"Please?" Alli asked again, leaning intently toward her mother. "It will be fine. They are nice people."

"Alli, please, not right now," Beverly said through clenched teeth. "Let's just get back to enjoying our evening."

With a renewed intensity, Alli said, "We've come this far. I've done so much research. Why not say something?"

Ruth carefully studied Alli's actions. "Wait. Say nothing more. Give me a minute. I need to get someone over here." Ruth left the table and brought

Rocco back with her, almost dragging him across the dining room.

"This is Rocco Montalvo," Ruth said hurriedly. "He has a photograph I'd like you to look at, Alli. Please show her the photo."

"The one from the museum?" Rocco asked.

"Yes. The one you sent in my email."

Even as he fumbled with his phone, he said, "Certainly, Ruth. But I don't understand. Here it is. Who needs to see this?"

Ruth handed the phone to Alli. "Do you recognize anyone?"

Taking the phone and sliding her fingers to zoom in, Alli's mouth slowly opened. Her eyes widened. She looked from Rocco to Ruth to her mother.

Beverly reached for the phone. She pulled out a pair of white framed reading glasses and peered at the photo. All eyes were on her. Alli stood and moved behind her mother's seat, looking over her shoulder.

"Where did you get this?" Beverly asked, her eyes never leaving the cell phone screen.

Rocco explained he was doing research for a friend. "A helpful museum curator provided this photograph for me."

Betty leaned over to see the photo on the screen. "Looks like an old photo. I love the theater. We should start it up again here in Harmony. Don't you agree, Beverly? Maybe Alli could help us out and direct a play. I know she's more of a film person. But we'd all work with her."

"I think Beverly knows these actors," Ruth said. "Am I right?"

"Mom," Alli said. "I know you've seen this photograph before. There's a copy of it in your memoir. It's time."

CHAPTER TWENTY-NINE

everly reached for Ruth's hand. "I'm in this photograph. When I was just starting out in New York."

The room spun. My vision tunneled. I grabbed the back of a chair just as Rocco took my elbow to steady me.

Betty clapped. "Well now if that isn't a coincidence! Ruth, that's Beverly in a theater group from when she was young," Betty said, pointing at the photo. "I can see the resemblance. Don't you, Ruth? Beverly, you looked just as beautiful then as now."

Eunice shoulder-bumped Betty. "Give Rocco a chance to tell us about the photo."

Alli's hands rested on her mother's shoulders as she

asked, "Mr. Montalvo, which person in this photograph is the one you've been searching for?"

"I believe she's the actress in the prairie costume," Rocco said. "We've been searching for Caroline Smith who once lived in Florida. My museum contact probably gave me the wrong information. Or…"

Beverly clasped her hand to her throat. She looked back up at her daughter standing behind her.

"It looks like I've upset you," Rocco said. "Please forgive me."

"Mom?" Alli said. "May I tell them now?"

"Why are you looking for this Caroline Smith?" Beverly asked.

"Because she has a half-sister right here in Harmony!" Betty blurted out. "We're not supposed to let everyone know though. Ruth here knew about the girl all along. Didn't you Ruth? But we all just found out about it."

"That's right, Betty," Ruth said. "Beverly, can you tell us if Caroline is this actress's name?"

Beverly took a deep breath. She handed the phone back to Rocco. "That actress is Caroline Smith."

"Hooray," Betty shouted. "So, this is a good lead."

Beverly smiled at Betty. "Yes, it seems so. I knew her."

"You knew Caroline? Tell us about her," Betty said.

"She left her home because she found out she was

adopted and had been lied to about it. When her mother passed away, she realized how wrong she had been to leave in anger like that. How much it hurt her mother. So that young woman Caroline took a stage name and used it in her acting career. She married and had a lovely daughter."

"What is her stage name?" Ruth asked with a soft voice.

Beverly continued. "She uses her husband's last name, Turner, and her adoptive mother's first name, Beverly."

I heard gasps from everyone seated around the table.

Alli hugged her mother. "It was time, Mom. Everything will be okay."

"Please continue the story, Alli. How you ended up here in Harmony," Beverly said.

"Caroline Smith became Beverly Turner. I followed along as Mom wrote her book, *Becoming Beverly*, and grew interested in her life as a young woman. She wrote about the couple who raised her. About her happy middle-class upbringing. They never told my mom she was adopted. She learned about it when a distant family member unwittingly broke it to her. It crushed her and she rebelled by fleeing to the theater scene in New York."

I stood listening to my niece Alli as she told us the story of my sister.

"Getting out into the bigger world, she came to realize how blessed she was to have had the parents she did. How much love they gave her…"

"And how horrible it was of me to lash out at them and leave," Beverly added. "We reconciled just before they passed away within a year of each other. I was grateful for that."

"I questioned Mom about never searching for her birth parents. She knew the records were sealed, and she didn't have a burning desire to mount some big search," Alli said. "But I did, right Mom?"

"Yes, you did," Beverly said, smiling lovingly at her daughter. "I had stashed the boxes of Mom and Dad's personal things away, meaning to go through them someday. But I was busy with my career. Then marriage and my own little girl. I vowed to make her childhood as happy as mine was. As Alli said, I had no burning desire to find the people who had given me up. I could never understand doing that. But Alli kept saying how she was curious about it. Would I mind if she looked through the papers in case they held a clue?"

"And they did! Big time clues," Alli said. "I found letters from my mom's birth father. Somehow, he gained access to sealed court records. He found out who his child's adoptive parents were. My grandparents kept his letters hidden away. His written words told me of a man who did not want his daughter to be taken from him. He spoke of an affair. Small towns. A family the woman had. How she would not put them through a scandal of her own making."

"Was he a judge?" I asked.

Alli looked at me. "Yes, he was. How did you know?"

"And he lived in Harmony, Wisconsin?"

"He did. Now you know why I've been coming here," Alli said.

"She didn't tell me what she was up to until this trip." Beverly looked around at all of us before her eyes landed on me. "I only knew my birth father's name, Judge Josiah Bell. I visited his grave this morning."

As Alli and Beverly were telling their story, the reality of what it meant was sinking in for everyone around the table except Todd, who never knew about my missing half-sister.

"The historic photographs at Kay's B&B are of my father's family. But we still don't know who my mother was. Alli's right. You are the generation who might remember those times. My adoptive parents never told me the complete truth. I learned to understand they were doing what they thought was right. My birth father tried to reach me but was thwarted. I don't know if my birth mother is still alive. My dear daughter Alli has brought me here hoping we can find her. Perhaps this is the time to ask. Do any of you know who had the affair with Josiah Bell? The person who gave birth to me?"

"I do." Those two simple words came from Ruth.

Scott came up behind me and touched my arm. "Are you all right?"

I reached for his hand and held tight. "Scott, I'd like you to meet my sister, Caroline Turner."

Scott looked back and forth. So did all of the others seated here. My friends and family.

Alli's unblinking eyes stared at me. A smile pulled at her lips.

Beverly was speechless as Ruth reached her arm around her shoulder. "We do know your mother. Joanna Parker. She was my sister-in-law. And the woman standing there is her other daughter."

Alli let out a little scream as she ran around the table to me. "Can I give you a hug, Jackie?"

I pulled her to me. "Yes. But call me Aunt Jackie."

The End

ABOUT THE AUTHOR

Here are a few ways to reach me…I'd love to stay connected!

Please sign up for my monthly newsletter. I'll share things about my life…both personal as Brenda Felber and professionally as my pen name Suzanne Bolden.
Like/follow Suzanne on her Facebook page

If you follow me on these two, you'll be automatically notified when new releases are available.
Bookbub
Amazon Author Central

Check out my website www.suzannebolden.com

Thank you for reading my books. If you enjoyed them, a review is much appreciated!

ALSO BY SUZANNE BOLDEN

Katie Murphy Cozy Mystery Series

#1 Pour Decisions

#2 Pick Yar Poison

#3 Raising Spirits

#4 Auld Lang Stein

#5 A Wee Lepre-Con

#6 Paws for a Pint

7 The Elf Did It

#8 Matrimony and Malice

#9 Read Between the Lines

9 781948 064255